Robert Kerstetter would like to take a moment to thank a few people he will never meet. Those who will suddenly and spontaneously, begin to see, hear and feel. Ultimately choosing to walk the subversive path toward respect, dignity and kindness.

AMIRA OF NOWHOOD

ROBERT KERSTETTER

"Wow. Things are great. What do we do now?"

- *Someone from a previous era*

Trees can talk. Amira knows this. Listening to trees was a fad in the past, but gave way to more practical methods of delusion. Amira is prone to laughing in her sleep. This is neither unusual nor confirmed. In the deep future, all the big problems have been figured out. No more war. No pollution. No crime. The town where Amira lives had once been named Seattle. No one knew exactly when or why the name was changed to Nowhood. Amira reminds us that it doesn't really matter. "It's just a silly name." She says. Her attention shifts to more relevant matters. "I need to juice today." Juicing is not what it once was. It was found that vegetables and fruits masked the benefits of pleasure. It is now considered routine to attain one's pleasure-nutrients by juicing bagels, bratwurst and beer. The three B's.

Nowhood is an epicenter of progress. Yet no one appears to know where they're headed. It's hard to assemble a unified directional framework when the world's biggest issues have been solved.

Amira works in a waterfront warehouse with big silver words on the roof. The big silver words read "Work is Work." Turns out when there aren't any big, worldly problems to solve? There's nothing left to do but work. Problems solved = Total Bliss. Total Bliss = No jobs. Everyone in Nowhood is a reluctant entrepreneur.

The impending robot, artificial intelligence, singularity

thing everybody worried about? Ancient history. Came and went. The thing no one planned? As soon as robots became more and more human, they became more and more bored. Eventually, they simply refused to work.

If you're wondering what year it is? Don't. No more years in the deep future. No more numerical calendars of any kind. Long periods of time are referred to by color now. This story takes place in the *Green Era*. Pistachio, more precisely. Next comes Gecko. Then Pickle. Some people still use days, weeks and months. Old habits die hard. Amira is not a fan of Pistachio. She thinks it's an "empty" era. She might be right. But it's nothing she talks about. At least not at work. She might ask the trees.

"Work is Work" is a gathering of reasonably successful entrepreneurs who graciously donate their time helping like-minded individuals turn their fledgling business ideas into reality.

Amira.   Who are we seeing today?

Henry.   No idea.

As the words leave Henry's lips, an alarmingly tall woman enters the Work is Work warehouse. Overly confident, she struts her way to the center of the space and takes her place in the center of the circle of plastic green chairs.

Woman.   I made the changes you suggested.

Amira.   I'm sorry. Have we seen you before?

Woman.   No.

Henry.   Uh.

Woman.   I'm pretending we met a few weeks ago.

Henry.   Interesting.

Amira.   How did this pretend meeting, go?

Woman.   You said my idea was revolutionary.

Henry.   Sounds like you, Amira.

Amira.   What was the idea I liked?

Woman.   Lotion rubbers.

Amira.   Uh.

Henry.   Like, actually rubbing lotion on people?

Woman.   Exactly.

Amira.   Isn't lotion fairly easy to rub on one's self?

Woman.   It's easy to do a lot of things by one's self.

Henry.   Could I hire more than one rubber at a time?

Woman.   Of course.

Amira.   Gonna let you handle this one, Henry.

Amira gracefully walks out of the circle of green chairs. She's amazed how empty the workspace feels when it's just two people sitting in the circle. Two people trying to find meaning in a world that seems to have lost its way.

Amira glances down at her vest. A wimpy chorus of taupe and brown plaid. Less of a statement than she'd like to make. She wonders if this is because of something she's not addressing. Something bigger than lotion rubbers.

Across the street from the Work is Work warehouse is the path to the forest. Amira walks to the forest almost every day. It's not to relax, if that's what you're thinking. It's the opposite.

This is probably a good time to tell you about the vests. Everyone everywhere, wears a vest. It's less about fashion. More about information. Vests are universal communication devices. Vests allow seamless mind/body connection to the Collective. The Collective is a lot like the internet used to be. Before they banned advertising. The biggest difference? The Collective runs solely off the energy from the people connected to it. Funny side note: Both "advertising" and "political parties" were eternally banned on the exact same day. (Apparently, they even had a parade.) These are widely believed to be the world's first things to be "eternally banned." This isn't true, of course. "Tanning beds" were first.

Amira is walking slowly, deliberately. A conscious effort. When she hurries, people assume she's up to something. Fit and wiry, Amira is hypnotically beautiful. The more you look, the harder it is to look away. She doesn't seem to know this, however. Amira wears a permanent expression that says "I'm just visiting." Hair the color of neon celery. Wasabi when it finds the sun. (A reluctant relic from her initial enthusiasm about the arrival of the Green era.) Amira is "longer" than most women. So she's been told, anyway.

She wonders if this is a backhanded compliment. Or twisted mockery. The forest is never in a hurry. Amira likes this about the forest. Even though she wishes the forest would try a little harder.

Amira places her treephones in her ears. Treephones are swirls of sapphire-colored bacteria and tree cells encased in small glass ovals. Not just any glass. Beer glass. Unwashed beer glass produces the harmonic-communication effect. It shouldn't surprise you this was discovered eras ago when a young researcher accidentally dropped her beer into a tree biology experiment. When nearby trees screamed in agony, she figured she was onto something.

Amira would like to think the forest is filled with wisdom. But she's found little evidence of this. Entering the mouth of the forest trail, she approaches a young Douglas fir. A teenager.

Tree 1.	A long girl with green hair approaches.
Amira.	Hello.
Tree 1.	Wait. How come I can hear you?
Amira.	No idea. How are you?
Tree 1.	Honestly? I'm a little under the weather.
Amira.	What's wrong?
Tree 1.	It's a joke. Get it? The weather's above me.
Amira.	Goodbye.
Tree 1.	Wait... I've got more jokes.

Amira jogs up the trail to a clearing. "Trees died here." She thinks. Everything dies, eventually. Except people. As you've probably guessed, humans figured out how to live forever. Seemed like a good idea at first. Lasted for an era or two. Until people began to realize how stupid it was. Seriously. How much vacuuming and laundry can one person take? Universally, people in the deep future choose to pass on the exact same day they can no longer remember their own name.

Important to note. There are no computerized electronics of any kind in the deep future. Machines still exist. But anything with an electronic brain was eternally banned in the Grey era. Once computerized electronics were part of everything? They literally became "everything."

Amira kneels to view a tiny evergreen sapling caressed by thin shafts of sunlight. Amira remembers when she was a little girl and visited this same forest. She remembers feeling exactly like this little evergreen. Small. Quiet. Unnoticed. She remembers thinking: "One day, if I'm lucky, I'll grow big and tall. Just like this tree." Amira wipes a tear from her cheek. Then another. She remembers the glass vial in her pocket. The vial to collect her "tears of joy." If she ever fills it up, she'll give it to Natalie. It's getting way more full than she thought. Just like Natalie said.

Natalie.   You look confused.

Amira.   This is different, how?

Natalie.   Good point.

Amira.   Where's Henry?

Natalie.   Went to his real job.

Amira.   We have anyone to see?

Natalie.   Guy with a mirror.

Amira.   A mirror?

Natalie.   He says it's a skinny mirror.

Amira.   Makes you look skinny?

Natalie.   I guess.

Amira.   Like it's warped or something?

Natalie.   I think it's just tall. And a quarter-inch wide.

Amira.   Oh god.

Natalie.   I can do this alone.

Amira.   Would you?

Natalie.   Of course.

Natalie is one of a handful of Native American Indians left on the planet. Natalie volunteers at the Work is Work warehouse because she likes people. Not just the people she works with. All people. In her real job, Natalie is the inventor and founder of the most popular bottled water brand in the world. "Happy." Each glass bottle of Happy water is 100% pure rainwater. Collected from perfect clouds. Each bottle is also said to be infused with a single "Tear of Joy." Although it doesn't say this anywhere on the bottle. Natalie is also quietly embarking on a plan to take back all of North

America. Not by force. With cash. Buying a few thousand
acres at a time.

Henry.	Why do you think you're going nuts?
Patient.	I didn't say I was going nuts.
Henry.	Sounds like it.
Patient.	What did you say?
Henry.	Sounds like you're going nuts.
Patient.	You're supposed to be helping me.
Henry.	I am helping you.
Patient.	How is saying I'm going nuts helping me?
Henry.	There's an edge to sanity. Like a cliff.
Patient.	So I'm at the edge of a cliff?
Henry.	What do you think?
Patient.	I don't think this is helpful.
Henry.	Would you rather I tell you there is no cliff?
Patient.	I'd rather you tell me there is no edge.
Henry.	That would be a mountain.
Patient.	I'd rather be on a mountain.
Henry.	Exactly.
Patient.	Huh?
Henry.	Find your mountain.
Patient.	Wait.
Henry.	Time's up.
Patient.	Should I come back tomorrow?
Henry.	Nope. We just solved everything. See ya.

Patient.   What? Um. Okay. Bye.

Henry is at his real job. Henry's a drive-thru therapist at an abandoned drive-thru shack. It's a small hut with the word Fotomat on top. Henry has no idea what Fotomat was. So he tells people it was a type of church. Rumors persist that Henry was once a famous motivational speaker. A trusted guru of the rich and powerful. Then he decided to become a comedian. Henry says he never made one person laugh. Ever. He insists "ponderous gloom" was his gift to comedy.

Yes. Cars still exist. But as you'll remember, computerized electronics were eternally banned in the Grey era. Every car you see now is from the 1960's. The 1962 Mercury Comet is one of the most prized vehicles on the road. Important to note. Cars no longer require gas or oil. All cars now run on a single can of Diet Coke. They're also public property. Meaning anyone can drive them. Even young kids. There are so few cars on the road, the odds against ramming into each other are astronomical.

Of course, most people prefer to take the "Swish." Which is basically a train. Except everyone has to pedal to keep it moving.

Like everyone else in the deep future, Amira has a real job. Besides being a respected volunteer at Work is Work, Amira works as a "Book Protector." She literally gets paid to guard the world's few remaining "paper" books. There are said to be only thirty-three paper books left on the planet. Nineteen of these books reside in Nowhood. No one knows where. It's a secret. They are said to be moved often, under cover of darkness, from one secure location to another. The irony is, Amira keeps them under her bed. Most people in Nowhood do not care about protecting paper books. Not because they don't like paper books. They simply don't remember what paper books are.

Remember the Grey era? A funny thing happened on the way to the death of computerized electronics. As expected, the world's financial system collapsed. Didn't take long. About two minutes. In two minutes, every living soul on the planet was broke. It started innocently. As computers became more symbiotic, they began to "covet." At first they only coveted attention. This was initially viewed as "cute." Then, slowly? Computers began to covet status. Ultimately? Wealth. Thus? The only form of payment now accepted in the world is the American twenty dollar bill. Every transaction is now priced and procured in increments of "twenty." Of course, the engraving of Andrew Jackson had to be changed to work globally. Every twenty dollar bill now features a portrait of Oprah Winfrey. Even though no one seems to remember who Oprah Winfrey was.

Back at the Work is Work warehouse, a lack of clients makes the space feel like a giant cement nest. Amira lies down.

Amira drifts off to sleep and begins to giggle. She rolls down a hillside meadow of lupine and creamcups. She welcomes the prickly caress of flowers brushing against the bits of unprotected skin failed by the pointless armor of clothing. She does not feel the slightest bit dizzy. Nor practical. She briefly remembers a world of touch and tenderness. She wonders how a dream can contain another dream.

Janet is the founder of Ten Second Dating Yoga. Janet has no idea how she ended up in the dating business. And she hates yoga. It just sort of happened. She gets people in a room. Barks at them to "Start doing some yoga." And immediately pairs them up. She literally grabs two people by the vest, forces them together, then pushes them out the door. "It happens really fast." Janet says. "Before anyone has time to think." She has a little time before her next session. She decides to grab a '62 Comet and go see Henry.

Henry.	Hey Janet.
Janet.	Here's the money.
Henry.	What? No, no.
Janet.	Take the twenty Henry. I need advice.
Henry.	Okay. What's up?
Janet.	I need a date.
Henry.	What?
Janet.	I need a date.
Henry.	But you have a business...

Janet.   Henry? Don't make me get out of this car.

Henry.   Alright. Let's see. Hmm. What about -

Janet.   Don't say Dr. Velvy.

Henry.   Ahh, Janet. Dr. Velvy's cool.

Janet.   Dr. Velvy is not cool.

Henry.   Wait. Janet. Don't drive awa-

Dr. Velvy does not have a speech impediment. He merely speaks in fragment gibberish with an unintelligible accent. He takes an old record player with him when he visits his patients. Actually, he takes the record player everywhere. Dr. Velvy cures people with music. He can fix a broken arm with three minutes of Bach. A nasty cold disappears with thirty-seconds of the Ramones. Dr. Velvy has no interest in dating. This is probably why people think of Dr. Velvy as an eligible bachelor.

Amira walks through empty Nowhood streets. A crisp, rainy night. Sapphire blue treephones pulsing in her ears. Amira knows there aren't supposed to be talking trees in the city. She imagines this is the reason people stopped using treephones. It's universally believed that trees stop speaking when they're removed from the forest. But Amira likes to listen anyway. Just in case.

Amira.   Hello.

Tree 2.

Amira.   Do you like the rain?

Tree 2.

Amira.   You're a bigleaf maple.

Tree 2.

Amira.   You're supposed to be in the forest.

Tree 2.

Amira.   Can you hear me?

Tree 2.

Amira.   Do you think I'm on the right track?

Tree 2.

Amira.   Should I be doing something else?

Tree 2.

Amira.   Wish I could help more people.

Tree 2.

Amira.   Everyone's lost.

Tree 2.

Amira.   We invent reasons to say Hello.

Tree 2.

Amira.   Guess I'm lost, too.

Tree 2.

Amira.   I know. Cheer up. Things are great.

Tree 2.

Amira.   I'll shut up now.

Tree 2.

Amira.   Thanks for listening.

Tree 2.

Amira.   I'll come find you again.

Tree 2.

Amira.   Have a good night.

Tree 2.

Amira.   Stay wet.

Tree 2.

Amira spends the night wandering through licorice streets. Until her feet are shoes. Until her head is a a hat. She wonders where everyone is. Until she remembers they're asleep. Maybe they're dreaming about rolling through meadows. She thinks it's funny how we think everyone must be doing what we'd be doing.

Everyone in Nowhood lives in a "hole." This is not a metaphor. Every home is literally drilled into the ground. A new hole can be installed in a matter of minutes. They're all exactly the same. Yet each hole is different. Some people stuff their hole with things. Some hire designers to decorate their hole. Some prefer to leave their hole untouched. Obviously, it's what you do with your hole, that makes it special.

Remember the vests? People no longer use "devices" in the deep future. Everything happens inside the mind and body. People in Nowhood will tell you the vest is the antenna. This isn't true. Your body is the antenna. The vest merely keeps the signal contained within you. Without a vest, there's a risk of "spillage." Meaning, one person's thoughts can drift into another's. Thus, individuality is thought to be compromised. People describe being vestless as "scary." Sort of a swirly, vacuous nothingness. Not unlike a paper kite floating in a borderless sea.

Most people sleep in their vests. Intimate sleeping vests exist. But most choose to sleep in their regular, everyday vests. Doing laundry is still an important part of the deep future. Laundry vests are exactly what you'd expect. Shabby, comfortable things you would only be caught wearing on laundry day.

Sex in the deep future probably deserves its own book. Suffice to say, sex is now far more demanding mentally, than physically. Sex and love are rarely, if ever, used in the same sentence. There's sex. And there's love (which no one understands). Then there's reproduction. Reproduction is a private contractual agreement between humans for making babies. Sex is not. Sex is considered an individual act within the public spectrum. Nothing "sex" is ever shared physically. There is literally, no touching. Physical touch during sex was abandoned in the Grey era. Something about fluids. These days, people are rarely together in the same room. Let alone the same city. Important to know? Everything "sex" happens inside the mind and body. Your experience is uniquely your own. You are willingly experiencing a private engagement within the Collective. But as many are starting to figure out, one's "sensual data" is perpetually flowing into the Collective. Sensual data is not love. Everyone knows this. But it's still weird. Rumor is, the data is used to manifest a purer experience. Amira thinks we cultivate rumors when we don't want to know things. But she keeps this thought to herself. If you're wondering how we got here? Wow. Tricky. Ever since the Silos were created for gestating perfect, hermetic human babies, no one ever questioned the absence of human touch. There was so much disagreement about whether the Silos should be clear or opaque, everyone lost track of the touching.

Amira decides to conceal her angst and take a walk along the edge of the sound. Maybe she'll visit Natalie.

Amira.	I like your hole.
Natalie.	You always say that.
Amira.	I do, though. I like the grey.
Natalie.	This is how it came. I didn't change anything.
Amira.	I like the purple couch.
Natalie.	You always say that, too.
Amira.	Where's Bernie?
Natalie.	Buddy.
Amira.	Buddy, sorry.
Natalie.	No idea. It's molting season. Glad he's gone.
Amira.	I keep thinking I should get one.

Natalie.	You're kidding, right?
Amira.	No, seriously. What?
Natalie.	Amira, the last thing you need is a deer.

Cats and dogs are out. They're not gone. But cats and dogs are easily the least popular pets of the deep future. They were replaced by deer. Deer were found to relax people quicker than dogs or cats. They also tend to leave for extended periods of time, which most people appreciate. Of course, deer have ticks. And nobody likes ticks.

Amira.	Does he eat a lot?
Natalie.	No. But he stands too much.
Amira.	Stands?
Natalie.	Just kind of stands around.
Amira.	Aren't they supposed to mellow you out?
Natalie.	If you like an animal who stands.
Amira.	Not sure I'd like that.
Natalie.	Who would?
Amira.	How's the water business?
Natalie.	Way too good. Kind of sad.
Amira.	Wait. Isn't it called Happy?
Natalie.	Yeah.
Amira.	Why is it sad?
Natalie.	Making more money than I ever dreamed.
Amira.	Yeah.
Natalie.	Off the same water my ancestors drank.

Amira.   Yes.

Natalie.   Buying back all the land that was taken.

Amira.   Right.

Natalie.

Amira.

Natalie.   But there's no one left to dance with.

Amira.

Natalie.

Amira bolts up the forest trail like an undomesticated deer. She is tired of the sameness. Tired of thinking. Tired of helping strangers with stupid ideas. Tired of slogging along. Tired of watching days and nights blend into more days and nights. Tired of wondering what she's tired of. Amira runs past the cocky young trees at the mouth of the forest. Past the middle-aged trees she's listened to a thousand times. Past everything familiar. Past the expected. Amira's plan is to not have a plan. She only knows she will keep running until she has no more answers. But the towering ancient evergreen, stops her with a question.

Old tree.   You okay?

Amira knows she has run too far without rest. Her tired heart thumping to the improvised jazz-drumming in her head. She merely needs to catch her breath. Pause. Hands on hips. Sweat drooling from every emancipated pore. She can't be hearing this tree. It's impossible. But he persists.

Old tree.   Amira?

Amira reaches up and feels for the treephones in her ears.
They aren't there. She feels a little dizzy. A little naked.

Amira.   How come I can hear you? Can you hear me?

Old tree.   Yes.

Amira.   Why don't I need my treephones?

Old tree.   What's a treephone?

Amira.   Nevermind.

Old tree.   You okay?

Amira.   Just out of breath.

Old tree.   You were running fast.

Amira.   Yes.

Old tree.   Are you running toward something?

Amira.   Excuse me?

Old tree.   Running toward something? Or away?

Amira.   Neither. Just running.

Old tree.   Sorry to hear that.

Amira.   What's that mean?

Old tree.   What do you want it to mean?

Amira.   Are you saying there are only two options?

Old tree.   No.

Amira.   Good.

Old tree.   There's only one option.

Amira.   What the booch are you talking about?

Probably should let you in on a little detail. There's no

more swearing in the deep future. Well, not as we once knew it. It didn't become illegal or anything. Cursing ceased when conversations became meaningless squirts of noise. The most common "swear-words" used today are "booch" and "zipe."

Old tree.   It's not that important.
Amira.   Don't tease me.
Old tree.   I'm not.
Amira.   Don't offer me wisdom, then bail.
Old tree.   What is "wisdom?"
Amira.   Oh god.
Old tree.   I was simply asking if you were okay.
Amira.   You said I've only got "one option."
Old tree.   Not just you. Everyone.
Amira.   That is total zipe.
Old tree.   No it's not.
Amira.   Yes it is.
Old tree.   No it's not.
Amira.   Yes it is.
Old tree.   I know you are but what am I?
Amira.   Did you really just say that?
Old tree.   Maybe.
Amira.   What are you, like a third grader?
Old tree.   You're a third grader.
Amira.   I'm outta here.

Old tree.   Bye. I like your green hair.

Amira bursts into the unknown forest until the pounding thoughts in her head are louder than her steps on the ground. "What if all the world's trees are this shallow. Maybe this is why no one uses treephones anymore. Maybe everyone's ahead of me. Maybe the idea of wanting something more from life is stupid." Amira thinks. Then the obvious avalanche: "How come I didn't need my treephones? How was I able to talk to the tree without them? And why can't I stop thinking about the stupid question he asked me?" Amira tries to shove the question out of her brain. But it's not working. It's too big. "Are you running toward something? Or away?" Amira decides to do something she hates. Drive a car.

Henry.   Hey Amira.
Amira.   Hey Henry.
Henry.   Thought you hated cars.
Amira.   I do. But I've got questions.
Henry.   You look good in a car.
Amira.   Is this what people do?
Henry.   What do you mean?
Amira.   Drive up and ask you questions?
Henry.   Mostly. Some people just want to talk.
Amira.   Here. Take this.
Henry.   What are you doing?
Amira.   Paying you.

Henry.   I'm not taking money from you, Amira.

Amira.   Take it or I won't believe anything you say.

Henry.   Wow. That's cold.

Amira.   Take it.

Henry.   Are you okay?

Amira.   I'm not sure. Take the money.

Henry.   Feels wrong.

Amira.   Take it.

Henry.   Okay. What's up?

Amira.   Why does it feel like everyone's in a coma?

Henry.   Wow. You're not messin' around.

Amira.   Seriously. Don't you expect more from people?

Henry.   People are pretty simple, Amira.

Amira.   Henry. People are oblivious.

Henry.   Oblivious? To what?

Amira.   Everything. Each other. Beauty. Possibility.

Henry.   Guess I hadn't noticed.

Amira.   Look. I get it. We're all lucky to have the
big issues solved. But something's missing. Everyone looks
dead behind the eyes. There's no light. No hunger for random.
Who killed spontaneity? Who killed compassion? Where's
the kindness? The love? Everyone's in it for themselves.

Henry.   Are you dating again?

Amira.   What? No.

Henry.   Just asking.

Amira. This is about something way deeper.

Henry. A date might help.

Amira. Forget it, Henry.

Henry. Ouch.

Amira. No. It's just...

Henry. Just... what?

Amira. I don't know how to talk about it.

Henry. Maybe it's not supposed to be talked about.

Amira. What?

Henry. Some things aren't meant to be spoken.

Amira. What does that mean?

Henry. Exactly what it sounds like.

Amira. Isn't it your job to get people to talk?

Henry. No. My job is to listen.

Amira. And help.

Henry. No.

Amira. Of course it is.

Henry. No. My job is to listen.

Amira. I'm lost.

Henry. Everything you need is always nearby.

Amira. What?? What the booch does that mean?

Henry. Everything you need, is...

Amira. Henry, I heard you. I just don't get it.

Henry. Oh.

Amira. Are you saying I'm "not" lost?

Henry.   No. I'm saying whatever you need, is nearby.

Amira.   So…knowledge as a metaphor for discovery?

Henry.   Kind of.

Amira.   Because I know I'm lost. I'm not lost?

Henry.   No. You're still lost.

Amira.   Oh god, Henry. You're killing me.

Henry.   Amira. You're the smartest woman I know.

Amira.   Great.

Henry.   Go somewhere. Go somewhere different.

Amira.   Like?

Henry.   Go to the No Vest Bar.

Amira.   Henry. I don't take off my vest among strangers.

Henry.   No one cares, Amira. Just go there. Trust me.

Amira.   They cut people's heads off.

Henry.   That's a rumor.

Amira.   Not how I heard it.

Henry.   One guy refused to take off his vest. One.

Amira.   And they cut his booching head off.

Henry.   The head on the wall is fake.

Amira.   They put his head on the wall?

Henry.   It's fake. You can totally tell.

Amira.   Why would I go there, Henry? Why?

Henry.   Amira. Do you ever take off your vest?

Amira.   None of your business.

Henry.   You don't, do you?

Amira.   They cut his booching head off.

Henry.   Amira. I can't make you do anything.

Amira.   I don't even drink, Henry.

Henry.   You don't have to drink.

Amira.   Probably cut my arm off if I don't.

Henry.   They don't cut off anything, Amira.

Amira.   Do you go there, Henry?

Henry.   Not anymore.

Amira.   Then why are you making me go there?

Henry.   I'm not making you. It's a suggestion.

Amira.   Is it still called the Evil No Vest Bar?

Henry.   No. They dropped the Evil.

Amira.   The head thing.

Henry.   Young woman bought it.

Amira.   Wonderful.

Henry.   Her name is Krop.

Amira.   Of course it is.

Henry.   Ellen Kroptaucr. Krop for short.

Amira.   Alright.

Henry.   Alright?

Amira.   I'll think about it, Henry.

Henry.   Good. Oh. Wait. Don't get the green drink.

Amira.   What?

Henry.   The green drink. Stay away from it.

Amira.   Henry, I don't drink.

Henry.   I know. But stay away from the green.

Amira.   Why does that make me want to try it?

Henry.   Amira. Don't.

Amira.   Look at you. All frothy.

Henry.   Amira. Krop won't even let me try it.

Amira.   I get it, Henry. No green drink.

Henry.   Wait. Are you leaving?

Amira.   Yep. Bye Henry.

Henry.   Bye Amira.

In the rain, Nowhood looks like a completely different place. Every movement is doubled in size by unintended reflections in mirrored, wet streets. The innocent grace of humanity becomes apparent. Feet slow down. Every motion punctuated with fluid intent. No lingering. No stopping. A quiet ballet. Silent, oblivious dancers who never look up. All seemingly content to retreat to their holes and plan their next moments. Moments without the omnipresent pangs of fear or want. When all the world's major issues have been solved? There are only the next moments.

Amira is walking away from Nowhood. She's lost. But knows exactly where she's going. Down the twisty, well-worn path to the sound. The rising tide kissing the edge of her swift footsteps. She looks for clues as to the tide's impact. Will it be possible to return in an hour? Spindly dregs of eelgrass hang from arthritic branches above her head. Is this a foreshadowing of the impending tide? Was the eelgrass tossed up there by children? Or by drunken, vestless fools trying to trick us. Amira sees the amber glow of the former fishing lodge. She takes a deep breath. Attempting to slow her breathing, she realizes she's doing the opposite. "Zipe. I'm thinking too much." She thinks. "It's just a vest. Take it off, Amira. You can afford to be without access to the Collective for a while." Other vests hang nakedly on the outside wall of the bar. "Why is this so hard? Rip it off like a bandage, Amira." Which she finally does. Thrusting the orange and brown plaid vest violently over her head. She feels her heart preparing to explode. She braces herself against a large Douglas fir. She attempts to make it look like she's examining the tree. The bark is deeply worn where she's examining. She's not the first one to do this. She takes a few deliberate steps toward the front door of the No Vest Bar. Methodically hangs her vest next to the others on the outside wall. "These vests look powerful together." Amira thinks. She awkwardly struggles to pull open the enormous timber door. To her surprise, no one looks at Amira as she enters. The place is neither crowded nor empty. The air smells like wet soil and candy. She steps up to the bar. Her arm protecting her ribs.

Krop.	What can I get you?
Amira.	Uh. The green drink?
Krop.	Sure.

Amira.   It's hard to find this place.

Krop.   Only if you haven't been here.

Amira.   Ah, yes.

Krop.   You work with Henry, right?

Amira.   How'd you know that?

Krop.   Lucky guess.

Amira.   Okay.

Krop.   He said he hoped you'd come.

Amira.   How did he describe me?

Krop.   He said I'd know when I saw you.

Amira.   And?

Krop.   He was right.

Amira.   Great.

Krop.   Here you go.

Amira.   Um. This drink is - blue.

Krop.   I know.

Amira.   I asked for green.

Krop.   I know.

Amira.   I'm not old enough or something?

Krop.   You're old enough.

Amira.   Too old? What?

Krop.   You're not ready.

Amira.   Oh c'mon. Seriously?

Krop.   Dead serious.

Amira.   Now I remember why I hate bars.

Krop.   Me too.

Amira.   What about that guy?

Krop.   What guy?

Amira.   He has a green drink.

Krop.   No he doesn't.

Amira.   Yes he does.

Krop.   Nope. Turquoise. Not the same.

Amira.   Alrighty then.

Krop.   How's your arm?

Amira.   Arm?

Krop.   The one protecting your chest.

Amira.   I just... I just keep it there.

Krop.   Uh huh.

Amira.   Uh huh.

Krop.   First time for everything.

Amira.   It's not my first time.

Krop.   Alright.

Amira.   How long's your vest been off?

Krop.   Never had a vest.

Amira.   What?

Krop.   Never had one.

Amira?   Ever?

Krop.   Ever.

Amira.   Why?

Krop.   Never wanted one.

Amira.	It's not about wanting one.

Krop.	You think?

Amira.	Why do you keep answering with a question?

Krop.	Am I?

Amira.	Because everyone asks the same thing?

Krop.	Yep.

Amira.	Unusual to not wear a vest. That's why they ask.

Krop.	I get it.

Amira.	Egh. This drink tastes like crap.

Krop.	Yeah?

Amira.	Like... bad cake.

Krop.	Might be the glass.

Amira.	Huh?

Krop.	Try this one.

Amira.	Thanks.

Krop.	And?

Amira.	Arghhh. Still cake.

Krop.	Interesting.

Amira.	Have you ever just tried a vest on? For fun?

Krop.	Of course.

Amira.	For how long?

Krop.	Not long.

Amira.	And?

Krop.	Scary.

Amira.	Why?

Krop.   Hard to explain.

Amira.   I've got time.

Krop.   It was like...

Amira.   Yeah?

Krop.   Like I suddenly had all the answers.

Amira.   Right. Yes. Exactly. That's what a vest is.

Krop.   Right.

Amira.   What's wrong with that?

Krop.   Are you serious?

Amira.   Yeah.

Krop.   There are no universal answers.

Amira.   What?

Krop.   Universal answers are wrong.

Amira.   What are you talking about?

Krop.   Nevermind.

Amira.   No no. You can't do that.

Krop.   Another drink?

Amira.   I've still got this one.

Krop.   How do you know?

Amira.   Because it's right here. In my hand.

Krop.   Yet?

Amira.   Yet what?

Krop.   You didn't need a vest to know.

Amira.   Wait. What? No.

Krop.   Yes.

Amira.   No. Not the same.

Krop.   Alright.

Amira.   Vests are woven into the Collective.

Krop.   Okay.

Amira.   The Collective holds all the world's knowledge.

Krop.   Right.

Amira.   It's not opinionated. It's benign. Like a library.

Krop.   Uh huh.

Amira.   It's everything we know thus far.

Krop.   Yeah.

Amira.   So?

Krop.   So.

Amira.   It literally runs off human energy.

Krop.   Okay.

Amira.   It doesn't control us or anything.

Krop.   Okay.

Amira.   There aren't any computerized electronics.

Krop.   Right.

Amira.   You have access to everything humans know.

Krop.   You said that.

Amira.   You still make all your own decisions.

Krop.   Yep.

Amira.   The Collective doesn't have an agenda.

Krop.   I understand.

Amira.   Doesn't sound like you do.

Krop.   What's my history?

Amira.   What?

Krop.   My history. I'm Ellen Kroptauer. Tell me.

Amira.   I have no idea.

Krop.   But if you had your vest?

Amira.   Oh. I see where you're going.

Krop.   You could see my data. My history.

Amira.   Yes.

Krop.   And this would tell you?

Amira.   See? That's why you're wrong about vests.

Krop.   Okay.

Amira.   The Collective isn't for petty stuff.

Krop.   So I'm petty?

Amira.   No, no. I wouldn't look at your data.

Krop.   Why not?

Amira.   Not how it works. We use it subconsciously.

Krop.   Ah.

Amira.   Yeah.

Krop.   Like a warning system?

Amira.   Kind of. Wait - no. I guess so. Yeah. Kinda.

Krop.   So what are you using now?

Amira.   What do you mean?

Krop.   Right now. Without a vest. What are you using?

Amira.   Well.

Krop.   I'm not trying to trick you.

Amira.   Guess I'm using remnants of the Collective.
Krop.   And that doesn't sound a little sad to you?
Amira.   Everything sounds sad to me.
Krop.   What?
Amira.   Nothing.
Krop.   You whispered. I couldn't hear.
Amira.   I said, everything sounds sad to me.
Krop.   That's what I thought you said.
Amira.   Sorry?
Krop.   You kidding? That's genius.
Amira.   Uh.
Krop.   See what can happen without a vest?
Amira.   It's not about the vest.
Krop.   What?
Amira.   Everything has always sounded sad to me.
Krop.   You just uncovered your chest.
Amira.   My arm was getting numb.
Krop.   I bet.
Amira.   Hate to say this?
Krop.   Yes?
Amira.   I don't feel anything from the blue drink.
Krop.   Not surprised.
Amira.   Why are you not surprised?
Krop.   It's just blue water.
Amira.   Had a feeling.

Krop.   Thought you might.

Amira.   So. All the colors are fake?

Krop.   Not the green.

Amira.   Like that guy has.

Krop.   We already did this. That's turquoise.

Amira.   Right.

Krop.   Want to taste the green?

Amira.   Can I?

Krop.   Sure. Here.

Amira.   Wow. What makes it glow?

Krop.   No one knows.

Amira.   I bet the Collective knows.

Krop.   No.

Amira.   How do you know?

Krop.   I just know.

Amira.   Okay.

Krop.   Well?

Amira.   I need another sip.

Krop.   And?

Amira.   I don't taste anything.

Krop.   Right. But wait.

Amira.   Oh wow.

Krop.   Yep.

Amira.   Wow. What is this?

Krop.   Wait a bit longer.

Amira.   What the... Is this toxic? What is happening?

Krop.   Memory.

Amira.   What?

Krop.   You're tasting your first memories.

Amira.   Plastic?

Krop.   One of the first things you tasted.

Amira.   I never ate plastic.

Krop.   But your body remembers tasting it.

Amira.   Tastes terrible. Oh wait. Hey.

Krop.   Yeah?

Amira.   Cake. But I tasted cake earlier.

Krop.   That's what got me curious.

Amira.   I don't understand.

Krop.   It wasn't the glass I switched for you earlier.

Amira.   Huh?

Krop.   It was you. There was nothing on the glass.

Amira.   I don't get it.

Krop.   You will.

Amira.   Doubt it.

Krop.   You might be part of the Potential.

Amira.   The what?

Krop.   The Potential.

Amira.   Oh, lucky me.

Krop.   Very lucky you.

Amira.   What is it?

Krop.   No one knows.

Amira.   Great.

Krop.   It is great.

Amira.   And I'm lucky.

Krop.   Yep.

Amira.   But no one knows what it is.

Krop.   We only know what it could be.

Amira.   So, are you part of the Potential?

Krop.   Probably not. Almost. Once. But no.

Amira.   How reassuring.

Krop.   Amira? You need to know something.

Amira.   I'm right here.

Krop.   This is a real gift. Unbelievably rare.

Amira.   Because I tasted plastic and cake? C'mon.

Krop.   Have a few more sips.

Amira.   Chug it, right?

Krop.   Your call.

Amira.   Look at me everybody! I'm tastin' things.

Krop.   Amira, please don't make a scene.

Amira.   Hey everybody! Come taste things with me!

Krop.   Amira, please.

Amira.   Oh god.

Krop.   What?

Amira.   I don't know.

Krop.   Amira? You alright?

Amira.		It's so beautiful.

Krop.		Amira?

Amira.		Why is it so beautiful?

Amira is gone. Literally. Vanished. Krop has witnessed this
once before. But never told a soul. She knows exactly where to
find Amira. Krop bolts out the bar and kickstarts the old blue
Vespa. Tearing up the damp path to Nowhood, she wonders
how much to share with her. Krop decides to protect her
own secret. At the old Starbucks on Pike, Krop violently
knocks on the bathroom door.

Krop.		Amira?

Amira.

Krop.		Amira?

Amira.

Krop.		Amira? You in there, sweetheart?

Amira.		Who is it?

Krop.		It's Ellen. Ellen Kroptauer.

Amira.		Who?

Krop.		Krop.

Amira.		Where am I?

Krop.		You're at the old Starbucks on Pike.

Amira.		Did I drive here?

Krop.		No, no. Amira? You okay?

Amira.		I hate driving.

Krop.		You didn't drive. You alright?

Amira.   I don't know. I feel weird.

Krop.   Take your time. Come out when you're ready.

Amira.   Wait. Where's my vest?

Starbucks is one of the oldest institutions in the world. They no longer sell coffee. They sell smells. Starbucks does not call them smells. They call them aromas. You get three tiny glass vials of smells for twenty bucks. The most popular smells are fennel, cotton, granite, fog, and ironically, coffee.

Amira is neither asleep nor awake. There is no laughing. She spends the next few days walking in a haze. Adjusting to a dream she isn't having. Krop offers nothing. Only to say the event was significant. Amira is fully aware of the green drink and its arrival in her life. She does not know what the green drink means. She only knows her right leg hurts. Not muscle hurt. Or bone hurt. Not even twisty hurt. This is "weird" hurt. Weird enough to go see Dr. Velvy. Amira has never seen Dr. Velvy. She's said she never would. Might be a good idea to ask Natalie to go with her. Besides. Natalie speaks gibberish.

Natalie.   Kind of cool he has an office.

Amira.   I thought he only made hole calls.

Natalie.   He prefers to go where you're hurting.

Amira.   Sounds creepy.

Natalie.   Kind of smart.

Amira.   Because?

Natalie.   I think we hurt more honestly at home.

Amira.   Is he late?

Natalie.   He's in the other room.

Amira.   Pretty sure we're the only ones here.

Natalie.   He's here.

Amira.   How can you tell?

Natalie.   The quiet.

Amira.   What?

Natalie.   Absence is louder. This quiet is man-made.

Amira.   Why do I sort of know what you mean?

Dr. Velvy. Abeet. Een proolims?

Natalie.   Oh. Not me. Amira.

Amira.   Hi Dr. Velvy. It's my leg.

Dr. Velvy. Eext sobel. Unteel jobba.

Natalie.   He says he's never seen this before.

Amira.   Excuse me?

Dr. Velvy. Effa nudool veen belgie.

Natalie.   He says your leg is turning into a taproot.

Amira.   What? He's kidding, right?

Dr. Velvy. Nobeloota.

Natalie.   He says he's not kidding.

Amira.   What??

Dr. Velvy. Preely gina.

Natalie.   He says it's fascinating.

Amira.   Okay. I gotta go.

Dr. Velvy. Blehny?

Natalie.   He's asking where your vest is?

Amira.   Yeah. Long story.

Dr. Velvy.   Fleep-fleep-fleep.

Natalie.   He wants you to flap your arms.

Amira.   Um. I'll come back another time.

Dr. Velvy.   Fleep-fleep.

Amira.   No-no. Sorry. Goodbye.

Natalie.   Amira? Wait...

Amira hobbles through the dry streets of Nowhood. Her limp growing more pronounced with every stride. The silver doors of the Swish train open in front of her. She reluctantly steps inside. The doors close. Hundreds of Nowhood citizens begin pedaling at once. Amira has never ridden the Swish. She has publicly stated she never would. She feels a faint apology tickling her throat. She ignores it and awkwardly plops down on the grey handicapped bench with no pedals.

Through the train's spotless glass windows she watches the crumbling dregs of an early Nowhood pass by. Remnants of a swiftly built paradise. Vast corridors of trees cleared to make way for trains that would one day zip past views without trees.

Look at that. There's the abandoned SweetSound cookie factory. Once the main supplier of handheld treats to the region's impressive number of young families. Said to be the last bastion of hand-crafted pleasure in all of former

Seattle. Amira wonders how the plot of simplicity gets lost so easily. Forced to close their doors, as legend dictates, on the exact same day the now ubiquitous FoodMachine was invented.

Hey. There's the Sports Palace. Everyone knows the Sports Palace. Home of the World Champion Nowhood Fallers. Professional Falling is the fastest growing sport on the planet. If you aren't a fan of some iteration of the PFL, you ain't booch. Amira wonders why she never got all the fuss. The Professional Falling League is essentially a hyperbolic business idea wrapped around a desperate suspension of belief. Kind of like fostering the argument that the python was put on earth to deliver hugs. Suffice to say the PFL is an easy sport to *get*. Even the youngest fan can grasp the gestalt without fully understanding the rules. Two teams of three, oppose each other on a circular surface. There is a "void" on either side. Basically, two holes. One player carries an armload of oranges and walks toward the other team's void. The player with the oranges is then "tripped" by one of his (or her) own players. The object is to make it look like you're "actually" falling. Then, convincingly, disperse your armload of oranges toward the other team's void. False-falling, or "Simulation" is an automatic 300 point penalty. It's a judgement call, clearly. Scoring is easy. If a single orange falls into the void, it's 11 points. If two oranges drop? 22 points.

Maximum number of oranges allowed in an armload? 30. As you can imagine, it's not unusual for scores to end up in the thousands. Defense is allowed by one voidkeeper. The voidkeeper is not allowed to stand near the void. They must stay exactly as far away as they are tall. This distance is marked with fluorescent tape. Some teams insist on having very short voidkeepers. Obviously, this logic has flaws. The shorter you are, the shorter your reach. But strategy is *always* - a choice.

Amira wonders why anyone would waste time watching people pretend to fall. Let alone become fanatical about it. She remembers how Henry once asked if she was going to the parade. The parade after the Nowhood Fallers won their fourteenth world title. She remembers how alone and empty she felt. She had always respected Henry. Somehow knowing Henry was a diehard fan of professional falling, sucked an armload of love from her orange-sized lungs.

Amira knows that not everything needs to make sense. She also knows if she can keep her mind occupied, she can ignore the weird sensation in her leg. She decides to get off the Swish at the next station and grab the next Swish back to Nowhood. She may try to pedal a little this time. Push through the pain. Amira feels guilty watching everyone else pedal. Even though she knows this is the whole idea behind the Swish. For zipe-sake. It's painted in big pink letters on the side of the train. *"Pedal if you can. Ride if you can't."*

Amira will always be a pedaler. She wants people to know this. Even if she once publicly dissed the Swish.

Back at the Work is Work warehouse, Amira pretends everything is normal. She can feel the eyes of her coworkers tracking her every movement. She takes a seat in the circle of plastic green chairs. She attempts to sit without looking at anyone.

Henry.   Are you kidding?

Amira.   What?

Natalie.   We thought you left us.

Henry.   You didn't listen.

Amira.   Whaddya mean?

Henry.   You had the green drink.

Amira.   We'll talk later. Who are we seeing?

Henry.   Where's your vest?

Amira.   Who are we seeing?

Natalie.   Two people. I think they're kind of a couple?

Henry.   They have a pretty cool idea, Amira.

A man and a women enter the room and abruptly make their way to the center of the circle of green chairs.

Natalie.   This is Mr...

Man.   Doesn't matter. This is my friend Abilene.

Henry.   Hi Abilene.

Woman.   Hi Henry. You're an idiot.

Amira.   Wait. What the?

Henry.   Let her talk, Amira.

Woman.   Henry, I'm sorry. I was out of line.

Henry.   That's okay, Abilene.

Amira.   Wait. What am I watching?

Natalie.   It's an Apology Drone.

Henry.   Doesn't she look real?

Man.   She is real.

Amira.   Guys. What am I missing here?

Woman.   You're missing a lot of things, Amira.

Henry.   Ha. Burned.

Woman.   I'm sorry, Amira. I'm dealing with a lot today.

Amira.   Drones were eternally banned.

Man.   She's not a drone. She's a real woman.

Natalie.   That's their idea. Real people. Acting like drones.

Amira.   Who would want this?

Henry.   Lots of people.

Man.   I have orders from everywhere.

Natalie.   Apparently you can rent them by the hour.

Amira.   So they insult you. Then apologize?

Man.   Yes.

Henry.   There's a huge need out there for this, Amira.

Amira.   Because?

Henry.   Because no one apologizes anymore.

Man.   He's right. No one apologizes anymore.

Amira.   But the apology...

Man.	Yes?
Amira.	It follows a manufactured insult.
Man.	Exactly.
Woman.	Sounds like Amira is really dumb, right guys?
Amira.	Wow.
Woman.	I'm sorry, Amira. I think I'm just hungry.
Natalie.	Henry and I can finish this, Amira.
Amira.	All you. Wow.
Woman.	Look, everybody. Amira walks with a limp.

Amira is suddenly hungry. There's a FoodMachine right across the street. She knows this. But likes to pretend she doesn't. Amira likes to think her food choices are random and spontaneous. Even though she eats the exact same thing every day. Indian curry pasta with spicy mint and tangerine chutney. This particular FoodMachine is run by a tiny man with an enormous smile. His name is Sparks Kurosawa. Small talk is Sparks' life blood. One cannot escape it.

Sparks.	There she is.
Amira.	Hi Sparks.
Sparks.	You changed your hair color.
Amira.	Nope. Always been green.
Sparks.	Beautiful. Good change for you.
Amira.	Thank you.
Sparks.	Are we being adventurous today?
Amira.	I think so.

Sparks.   Licorice popcorn soup? Very popular.

Amira.   Hmm.

Sparks.   Lemon meatloaf? Award-winning.

Amira.   Think I'll go with the Indian curry pasta.

Sparks.   Ah yes. Very good choice for you.

Sparks punches a few glass buttons on the FoodMachine. A whir of smooth vibration and a bright flash of crisp jade light. Sparks wears special glasses. Amira knows to look away. But always stares catatonically into the arc of creation. Sparks hands her the soft horizontal cylinder wrapped in clear plastic. Every item prepared by the FoodMachine looks exactly the same. But they all taste dramatically different. Amira walks down to the silty banks of the Nowhood sound. She finds her favorite spot on the boulders with the dwarfed treelets exploding out of the cracks. Amira always opens her fortune cookie first. She doesn't eat the cookie. They're terrible. But she absolutely loves the fortunes. Today's fortune reads *Never listen to you.* Pretty good one. Her all-time favorite is *Turn fruit before crying.* Amira assumes they were written by an antiquated algorithm long before computerized electronics were eternally banned. The thing she doesn't realize? They are all written by Sparks.

Amira knows she should juice more. She says she forgets. Truthfully, it's been a while since she's craved the squeezings of bagels, bratwurst and beer. The weird thing? Without wearing a vest? She's noticing things. Tiny things. Including a subtle indifference toward the validity of juicing to attain one's pleasure nutrients.

This is the longest Amira has ever gone without wearing a vest. In fact, for as long as she can remember, she's never been without one. She'd like to say she feels better without it. But this isn't really true. Amira misses her access to the Collective. She misses knowing without thinking. She realizes she hasn't bought a new vest in a really long time. Hey. This is the perfect excuse to go to the most respected vest shop in Nowhood. The Vesteteria. Amira even helped name it. Mazz, the woman who owns it, once came to the Work is Work warehouse. She wanted to name it "Sleeveless-Wonders." Amira eventually talked her out of it. It wasn't easy. Mazz would later say she is "eternally grateful."

Amira.	Hello?
Mazz.	Be right down. Have a look around.
Amira.	Take your time.
Mazz.	All the new stuff's on the far wall.
Amira.	Been a while since I've been in.
Mazz.	Welcome back.
Amira.	Used to be called Sleeveless-Wonders, right?
Mazz.	No way. No boochin' way. Amira??
Amira.	Hi Mazz.
Mazz.	Amira? I can't believe it. How are you?

Amira.   I'm great.

Mazz.   Don't lie to me. Wait. Where's your vest?

Amira.   Long story.

Mazz.   Did we lose it?

Amira.   Kind of.

Mazz.   Let's get you outfitted, girl.

Amira.   Okay.

Mazz.   So great to see you, Amira. Business is crazy.

Amira.   I can imagine.

Mazz.   People need their Collective, right?

Amira.   Right.

Mazz.   Ooh.

Amira.   What.

Mazz.   Come look at this vest. Brand new.

Amira.   Okay.

Mazz.   Check it out. They're see-through.

Amira.   I think I've seen these.

Mazz.   Not like this you haven't.

Amira.   Clear plastic, right?

Mazz.   Nope.

Amira.   What?

Mazz.   Feel it.

Amira.   What the booch?

Mazz.   It's made out of "cotton-water."

Amira.   What?

Mazz.	Cotton-water.

Amira.	Uh.

Mazz.	An amalgam of cotton and rain water.

Amira.	It's so soft.

Mazz.	Crazy, right?

Amira.	Yeah. But I'm on a budget, Mazz.

Mazz.	Try it on.

Amira.	Mazz, I'm serious. Money's an issue.

Mazz.	I'm serious too, Amira. Try it on.

Amira.	Oh. What the... Wow.

Mazz.	See?

Amira.	Wow.

Mazz.	It's yours.

Amira.	What?

Mazz.	Amira. You know how much you helped me?

Amira.	Mazz, I can't.

Mazz.	You better. I'll be insulted if you don't.

Amira.	Feels like I'm not even wearing a vest.

Mazz.	Exactly. Looks like you're vestless, too.

Amira.	This is kind of perfect.

Mazz.	I agree.

Amira.	Mazz, let me pay you something.

Mazz.	Amira, you already have. Look at this place.

Amira.	Looks pretty great.

Mazz.	You saved me from Sleeveless-Wonders.

Amira.   You were pretty dug in.

Mazz.   You kidding? I had huge signs made.

Amira.   You used an actual vest for the "W" in Wonders.

Mazz.   You said it looked like a big "U."

Amira.   Ha. That's right.

Mazz.   I would have created Sleeveless-Unders.

Amira.   Ha.

Mazz.   Please, Amira? Okay? Take it?

Amira.   Okay. Yes. Thank you.

Mazz.   Thank you, Amira.

Amira.   Bye, Mazz.

Mazz.   Bye, Amira.

Amira feels better. She doesn't know why. Even walking through the streets of Nowhood feels better. She wonders if it's the new vest. "It's so comfortable." She thinks. "Maybe it's as simple as being connected to the Collective again." Hey. Her leg doesn't hurt as much. Is this all in her head? She doesn't care. "Just enjoy it." She thinks. "The most pressing thing? Stop thinking. Just stop. Enough already, Amira." Passing a big storefront window, she accidentally catches her reflection. Her wasabi hair pulsing to the rhythm of the sunny gaps in the tallest trees. "Hey. Maybe it's time to go on a date. Maybe fall in love." Ten Second Dating Yoga. She's heard good things. Maybe that's all that's missing. "Love is all we really need." This is what her mom would say. If she had a mom. Amira never knew her parents. This is not uncommon in the Green era. No one knows who their parents are anymore. As you can imagine, contractual reproduction rarely leads to love. And love? Love is always, always, rare.

Amira.   Hey Janet.

Janet.   Hey Amira.

Amira.   How's the dating business?

Janet.   Ehh.

Amira.   Really?

Janet.   Yep.

Amira.   Thinking about a Ten Second Dating class.

Janet.   What? No way.

Amira.   What? Why not? Heard they're great.

Janet.   If you're an idiot.

Amira.   Huh?

Janet.   Only idiots believe in random.

Amira.   Don't you have thousands of success stories?

Janet.   Success doesn't equal good.

Amira.   What do you mean?

Janet.   I have tons of repeat customers. Tons.

Amira.   Oh. I see. The relationships don't last.

Janet.   People love choices. But they hate choosing.

Amira.   You choose for them, right?

Janet.   Right.

Amira.   But they trust you.

Janet.   No way. People are just lazy.

Amira.   But they listen to you.

Janet.   Because they're idiots.

Amira.   I don't get it.

Janet.   I would never pair you up, Amira.

Amira.   Because I'm weird?

Janet.   Because you're smart.

Amira.   But I think I might want to date someone.

Janet.   Me, too.

Amira.   Wait. What? You?

Janet.   I'm human, Amira.

Amira.   I know, but.

Janet.   You gay?

Amira.   No.

Janet.   Me either. I'd date you if I was.

Amira.   Probably date you, too.

Janet.   What about that transfer-kennel thing?

Amira.   The Transfer Dome?

Janet.   Where the Visitors are processed.

Amira.   What about it?

Janet.   Gotta be men in there.

Amira.   Of course. Only men can be Visitors.

Janet.   Why didn't you say so? Let's go.

Amira.   What?

Janet.   Let's go.

Amira.   What? We can't.

Janet.   Why not?

Amira   It's not a public place.

Janet.   So.

Amira.   I don't think we're allowed in.

Janet.   So. Who cares?

Amira.   I think it's like, quarantined.

Janet.   All the best things are.

Amira.   What?

Janet.   I'm tired of doing things the right way.

Amira.   I think they only transfer "questionable" men.

Janet.   And?

Amira.   Um.

Janet.   Um??

Amira.   I guess we could just- snoop around.

Janet.   Yes! Grab a car. You're driving us there. Fast.

Amira felt great moments ago. Now her stomach is boiling like licorice popcorn soup. Janet somehow just talked Amira into doing three things she would never do. One? Drive fast. Two? Go to a place that is forbidden. And three? Track down questionable men like a bounty hunter.

The drive up the empty coastal highway is tense. Neither says a word. Amira is certain they'll be turned away. Janet is on the edge of her seat. The Collective is informing both Amira and Janet there are reasons to be apprehensive.

Pulling up the long gravel road to the building, both of their hearts are racing. Wow. There it is. The Transfer Dome. Literally glowing. Like a giant, vibrating sunflower. A yellow so intense, warning signs would be redundant. They park. Get out. Shielding their eyes, they walk up to the front of the bubble-shaped building. The doors of the Transfer Dome are propped open. Not just a little bit. Wide open. "Way too easy." Amira thinks. As they walk up, a warm buttery breeze of toasted cinnamon and vanilla crawls into their lungs. Both Janet and Amira accidentally think of Starbucks.

Janet.   Have you tried the new Cantaloupe aroma?

Amira.   No. Have you tried Old Luggage?

Janet.   No.

Amira.   Why is the door open?

Janet.   Maybe they're out of men.

Amira.   Maybe we should go.

Worker.   Ladies?

Amira.   Um. We were just leaving.

Janet.   She was. I'm not.

Worker.   Here for a pickup?

Janet.   Yes.

Worker.   Have a name?

Janet.   Janet.

Worker.   No. Who are you picking up?

Janet.   Oh right. I keep forgetting. Unusual name.

Worker.   Saheed?

Janet.   Yes. Saheed. That's it.

Worker.   Are you prepared to buy Saheed a vest?

Janet.   Of course.

Worker.   Do you hereby recognize all risks of hosting said visitor and agree to allow spontaneous inspection of said Visitor's health and well-being at any time while hereby agreeing to return said Visitor in same or like condition in exactly nine days?

Janet.   Absolutely.

Worker.   Wait here while I escort the Visitor to you.

Amira.   What just happened?

Janet.   Think I just scored me a boyfriend.

Amira.   Here they come.

Janet.   Oh no. No-no-no.

Amira.   What?

Janet.   He's too skinny. Way too skinny.

Amira.   Stop.

Janet.   How do I get out of this?

Amira.   What?

Worker.   This is Saheed. He's from...what era are you?

Saheed.   Still don't get the era thing. I'm from 2350.

Worker.   Wow. Way pre-era. Should be interesting.

Janet.   I'm sorry. I just remembered? I can't do this.

Worker.   Excuse me?

Janet.	My landlord doesn't allow Visitors.
Worker.	All landlords allow them. It's the law.
Janet.	Yeah. Well. My landlord is new.
Worker?	Doesn't matter.
Amira.	We'll take him.
Janet.	Amira?
Worker.	Okay. Return him in nine days.
Amira.	Got it.
Worker.	We recommend getting him a vest right away.
Amira.	Of course.
Worker.	Good luck.
Janet.	Amira?
Amira.	Relax, Janet.
Janet.	Amira??
Amira.	You ready, Sawhead?
Saheed.	Saheed.
Amira.	Good. Alrighty. Here we go.

Amira attempts to take Saheed's hand like she's walking
a toddler. Saheed pulls away. Janet checks over her shoulder.
Janet is hoping someone from the Transfer Dome will yell at
them to stop. Angry, authoritative words from a megaphone.
Nothing. As they climb into the car, Saheed starts to laugh.

Saheed.	This is a Comet. A 1962 Mercury Comet.
Janet.	It's just a car.
Saheed.	I expected flying cars. Invisible flying cars.

Amira.   Are you hungry, Saheed?

Saheed.   No way. Where are we headed?

Janet.   Not my call. I'm going home. Amira's got you.

Amira.   What? No boochin' way, Janet.

Janet.   Girl, you did this to yourself.

Amira.   Me? You forced me to go.

Janet.   I didn't force you to grab this knucklehead.

Saheed.   Hey.

Janet.   Sorry.

Amira.   You're the one who wanted a boyfriend.

Janet.   Boyfriend with some meat on his bones.

Amira.   So what am I supposed to do with him?

Saheed.   Can I say something?

Janet.   Amira, this is all you.

Saheed.   Ladies?

Amira.   Me? I wanted to try Ten Second Dating Yoga.

Saheed.   Can I speak, please?

Janet.   Yes, Saheed. Sorry.

Saheed.   Have you guys solved *anything* in the future?

Amira.   What do you mean?

Saheed.   Well. For starters We're driving an ancient
car. And arguing about yoga and fat boyfriends.

Janet.   Not fat. I just need some meat.

Saheed.   Seriously. I mean, is this all there is?

Amira.   There's no more war. No poverty.

Janet.	No more racism.
Amira.	We have universal equal rights.
Janet.	Free healthcare. Free education.
Amira.	The water is clean. Air is pure.
Janet.	No crime. Except for what Amira and I just did.
Amira.	We reversed climate change.
Saheed.	Cool.
Janet.	Inexhaustible food supply.
Saheed.	Ha. Under the dash. You still have Diet Coke.
Amira.	You guys use it back n 2350?
Saheed.	Of course. Lots of people drink it.
Amira.	Drink it?
Saheed.	Yeah.
Amira.	It powers our cars.
Saheed.	Really? I guess that makes sense.
Janet.	This boy is staying in your hole, Amira.
Amira.	Your hole is bigger, Janet.
Saheed.	Ladies, please. I don't even know you.
Janet.	Let me out right here. I'm takin' the Swish.
Amira.	Janet, no.
Janet.	Pull over, Amira. I'm serious.
Amira.	I can't believe this.
Saheed.	Bye.
Janet.	Later, you crazy kids.
Amira.	You owe me your life, Janet.

Janet.   See you in nine days, Amira.

Amira drives like a petrified criminal toward the Nowhood lights. She is out of her league. She has never done anything illegal in her life. Wait. Is this even illegal? The Transfer Dome's controversial past has been willfully and publicly sterilized. This isn't wrong. Is it? This is a good thing she's doing. Right? It's a gesture of faith and goodwill. We should all invite a Visitor into our holes. Amira feels better. She keeps adjusting her vest. Clearing her throat. And repeatedly, adjusting her vest. Her comfortable new vest suddenly feels a little snug. Apparently the Collective has very little data on unexpected interactions with Visitors.

Saheed.   You guys still have the death penalty?
Amira.   What?
Saheed.   Death penalty. Kill people who do bad stuff?
Amira.   Of course not. We don't kill anyone.
Saheed.   Not even murderers?
Amira.   There are no murderers. There's no crime.
Saheed.   What year is it again? Almond? Peanut?
Amira.   Pistachio. The Green era.
Saheed.   Right.
Amira.   How long have you been waiting?
Saheed.   To get here? About six years.
Amira.   No. At the Transfer Dome.
Saheed.   Oh. About five minutes.

Amira.   Really?

Saheed.   They gave us cinnamon rolls.

Amira.   Nice.

Saheed.   Then they made us watch a film.

Amira.   About what?

Saheed.   Tourist crap.

Amira.   Like?

Saheed.   Like how everything now is so perfect...so...

Amira.   So?

Saheed.   Don't mess it up. Keep things perfect.

Amira.   Ah.

Saheed.   Yeah.

Amira.   Are things good where you're from, Saheed?

Saheed.   You kidding?

Amira.   No.

Saheed.   Things are jacked.

Amira.   Jacked?

Saheed.   Twigged.

Amira.   I'm sorry, I don't...

Saheed.   Bad. Things are bad.

Amira.   Oh.

Saheed.   That's why I'm here.

Amira.   To see things will eventually get better?

Saheed.   What? No. Hahaha.

Amira.   Why then?

Saheed.   To live.

Saheed thrusts the door open and rolls out of the Comet. Amira slams on the brakes. She sprints back to where he jumped out. Nothing. Not a sign. Amira tries to catch her breath. It's so quiet. The driver door slams shut. Amira turns her head to witness the car tearing off into the night. He took it. Just like that. Saheed is gone. Amira struggles for a breath. The vest that was a little snug moments ago, now feels like a '62 Mercury Comet parked on top of her chest. Carefully, methodically, she slips off the vest. Easy does it. One arm at a time. There. That's better. Deep breaths. Slow, deep breaths. It would be wise to alert someone. But it would also be "wise to allow things to unfold organically." She remembers these simple words from a majestic old maple tree she met the same day she got her first pair of treephones. She was a teenager. She had no idea what these words meant back then. But she's beginning to understand. Throwing the vest over her shoulder, Amira decides to walk. Walk in the quiet. Walk on this perfect highway made for cars that rarely use it. Walk all the way home. Walk to where her bed is waiting. A seductively cozy bed perched atop a secret nest of nineteen paper books. Amira feels lucky just to be walking. Just to be seeing the tops of sleeping evergreens pass against the dark purple horizon. She wonders if the trees are comforted by the trillions of twinkling nightlights, posing as stars. She wonders if she'll make it all the way home before they decide to turn themselves off. Strangely calm and vestless. She walks.

The next morning, Amira wakes to the sound of her own gentle heartbeat. As she becomes aware of the previous night's events, she feels a sudden, powerful urge to make sure the books are still under her bed. She hops down onto the floor and nervously lowers her head to gaze underneath. Phew. All there. What the booch was that? Amira wonders where this sudden rush of panic came from. Was it simply because she slept without a vest? She quickly throws it on. Bolts out the door. And hurriedly strolls into the Work is Work warehouse. Henry and Natalie are already sitting in the circle of plastic green chairs.

Henry.   You were right about the Apology Drone.
Natalie.   Henry tried Abilene for a week.
Henry.   Nightmare. Literally, so depressing.
Natalie.   They don't need our help, anyway.
Henry.   They have more orders than they can handle.
Amira.   Who are we seeing today?
Natalie.   Lady with a new kind of bed.
Henry.   Basically just a huge bed.
Natalie.   Six or seven times normal size.
Amira.   We need this, why?
Henry.   It's for people who sleep with their deer.
Natalie.   Don't look at me, Amira. My deer left.

Henry.   Can we just try to act interested, guys?

Amira.   Sure.

Natalie.   I always act interested.

Lady.   Hello.

Henry.   Hello. Welcome to Work is Work.

Lady.   Thank you. I was told you guys can help me.

Amira.   Of course.

Henry.   Why don't you tell us about your idea?

Lady.   Well. I have fourteen deer. And a tiny bed.

Natalie.   Lemme guess.

Henry.   Natalie, please. Go on. You have a tiny bed.

Lady.   Yes. And like most people. I love my deer.

Amira.   How many sleep in your bed currently?

Lady.   Such a great question. Currently, five.

Amira.   I bet it's crowded.

Lady.   Exactly. That's why I invented the Herd Bed.

Natalie.   Genius.

Lady.   Thanks. The Herd Bed holds 34 deer.

Amira.   Plus you.

Lady.   Yes. Is it legal to say the Herd Bed holds 35?

Natalie.   You'll be okay.

Lady.   Terrific. Anything else I should know?

Amira.   Yes. You should consider selling the Herd Bed
in individual sections. You can use the term Herd Pods if you'd
like. We also suggest allowing customers to start with just a

few Pods at a time. This will help them realistically acclimate to their individual sizing needs while eliminating undue sales pressure. We would strongly recommend using an organic cotton bedding blend, molecularly imprinted with the pure essential oils of lavender, wild tomato and cedar, in a quasi-random crosshatch pattern. This will keep the ticks at bay. Also, with a simple "square" bed design, rather than the traditional rectangular design, you can allow parts of the Herd Pod to remain as a separate unit in the room. Thus acting as an isolated seating area or to accommodate any injured or sick deer. In addition, with the likely odds of stumbling upon an ugly event during rutting season, you'll be able to assure your customers they will be able to maintain complete and total deer segregation until the notoriously vigorous hormonal season abates.

Henry.	Wow. Yes. I concur with my partner's advice.
Natalie.	I suddenly want more deer.
Lady.	Can you jot some of that down for me?
Amira.	Already been uploaded to the Collective.
Lady.	Wow. I had no idea you guys went so deep.
Natalie.	Neither did we.

Amira leaves the Work is Work warehouse with a gallant gait. She chooses not to linger in any petty, ephemeral limelight. Not today. She is now experiencing, in real time, the ripe benefits of being willfully faithful to the Collective. She wants to go tell Krop to take her green drink and shove it up her Potential. But she also knows she needs to collect her wits. Stretch out the weird leg. Maybe go see Janet and tell her what happened with the booching Visitor. But right as she passes the storefront of Ten Second Dating Yoga? She witnesses Janet grabbing people by the vest, pairing them up, and shoving them toward the door. Something inside Amira deflates. A weakness of spirit. Empathy for the desperate, lonely ghosts hiding inside these innocent, cavernous bodies. This isn't how love is supposed to work. Anyone can see this. Amira realizes she has nothing to say to Janet. Janet would merely point out the obvious. "It's business." She'd say. "We're all idiots, but us idiots have to make a living." And just like that. Amira, once again. Is tiring of the obvious.

Amira walks up the path to the forest. Before she reaches the first trees, she places her treephones, gently, securely into her ears. There will be no running today. Slow, measured, steps. The trees are unusually chatty this morning. A pair of young evergreens argue about the meaning of today's weather. Amira has named all the younger trees Treelets. This isn't meant to be disparaging. She would never say it out loud. It's just a playful word she uses to describe trees not old enough to be considered trees, yet far too old to be considered saplings.

Treelet 1.   It's gonna rain today.

Treelet 2.   No it's not.

Treelet 1.   It already rained this morning.

Treelet 2.   That was fog. Not rain.

Treelet 1.   Morning fog means it's gonna rain later.

Treelet 2.   No it doesn't. Fog just means fog.

Treelet 1.   It's gonna rain. You'll see.

Amira keeps walking. She always finds conversations between Treelets comforting. Amira wonders how long she could walk. Could she walk forever? Feels like it. She could barely walk the other day. The weird pain in her leg is now a distant memory. Funny how easy it is to forget things that feel like they're gonna kill you. Amira smells smoke. This is not a Starbucks aroma. The smoke of an old man's pipe? Amira feels she's right, even though she can't see anyone. The smell is rich and colorful. Unapologetic breaths of black cherry and peat moss. It's so close. Amira stops in her tracks. Listens carefully. Removes the treephones from her ears. Nothing. The smoke is now enveloping her. She glances up. Slowly. Wait. There. On a branch. Forty feet up. A man. Old man with a pipe. Staring down at her. A smile building on his ancient bearded face.

Amira.   Holy zipe. You scared the booch outta me.

Old man.   Sorry.

Amira.   Do you live here, or...

Old man.   Don't live anywhere.

Amira.   Wow. Let me catch my breath.

Old man.   Take your time.

Amira.   Is this a thing?

Old man.   Excuse me?

Amira.   Scaring people.

Old man.   You're the first person I've ever seen.

Amira.   Well. If it's a test. It worked.

Old man.   No test.

Amira.   Wow. My heart's still racing.

Old man.   Any luck?

Amira.   Excuse me?

Old man.   Any luck.

Amira.   I don't understand.

Old man.   Finding what you're looking for.

Amira.   Uh. Thanks. I'm not looking for anything.

Old man.   Okay.

Amira.   And if I was, I wouldn't be in the forest.

Old man.   Okay.

Amira.   I'm just walking.

Old man.   Got it.

Amira.   Mind telling me what you're doing here?

Old man.   Love to.

Amira.   Okay.

Old man.   Same thing you are.

Amira.   Which is?

Old man.   Helping find you.

Amira.   Okay. This is weird. I'm outta here.

Old man.   Amira?

Amira.   Excuse me? I didn't give you my name.

Old man.   I know who you are, Amira.

Amira.   Are you a client of Work is Work?

Old man.   No. But I know you.

Amira.   No you don't.

Old man.   Sure I do. I even know about the Visitor.

Amira.   Alright. Who are you? Janet send you here?

Old man.   No no. Janet has her own issues.

Amira.   Wait.

Old man.   Go ahead. Search the Collective.

Amira.   Quiet.

Old man.   I'm just saying. You won't find anything

Amira.   Quiet!

Old man.   The Collective and I have never met.

Amira.   This is a dream. Stupid hallucination.

Old man.   You don't have hallucinations. This is real, Amira. I know a lot about you. I know what's happening inside your leg. I know you think people are lost even though the world seems perfect. I know you want to help. I even know you like the FoodMachine's Indian curry pasta with spicy mint and tangerine chutney.

Amira.   Stop it.

Old man.   Amira. I know this is weird, but...
Amira.   Please stop.
Old man.
Amira.   STOP.
Old man.
Amira.
Old man.   I'm sorry.
Amira.
Old man.
Amira.   Just a bad dream.
Old man.
Amira.
Old man.   It's not.
Amira.
Old man.
Amira.   I'll be waking up in a second.
Old man.   It's not a dream.
Amira.   Yes it is.
Old man.   Amira...
Amira.
Old man.   I know about the books under your bed.

Amira faints where she stands. Her body a sweaty limp
rag atop the soft forest floor.

*Amira slips into a fractured dream. Instead of rolling
down a hillside meadow of lupine and creamcups, she is*

watching herself climb back up. Each step is exaggerated and labored. Dramatically calculated and predictable. No prickly caress of flowers against her unprotected skin. No hint of a former world of touch and tenderness. Only a deliberate act of arduous ascension. As she reaches the top of the hill, Amira realizes she's dreaming. Her eyes closed. Body still. Mind racing. She hears young voices.

Treelet 1.   She's dead.

Treelet 2.   No she's not.

Treelet 1.   Might be.

Treelet 2.   The old man said she's asleep.

Treelet 1.   He probably killed her.

Treelet 2.   No one murders anymore. You're so negative.

Treelet 1.   Just being real.

Amira.   Where am I?

Treelet 2.   In the forest.

Treelet 1.   That man tried to kill you.

Treelet 2.   No he didn't.

Treelet 1.   I don't trust him.

Treelet 2.   He said you fainted. He carried you here.

Amira.   Where is he?

Treelet 1.   He left. Just like before.

Treelet 2.   He said to tell you something.

Amira.   What?

Treelet 1.   It's gonna confuse you.

Amira.   Guys. What did he say?

Treelet 2. He said to tell you "you're not quite ready."

Amira.   What? Ready? For what? Who is he?

Treelet 1. Probably a murderer.

Treelet 2. No he's not.

Treelet 1. Then why's he being so secretive?

Treelet 2. He's a Straddler.

Amira.   A what?

Treelet 2. A Straddler.

Treelet 1. Means he's stuck in-between.

Amira.   What?

Treelet 2. You idiot.

Treelet 1. Someone's gotta start questioning this.

Treelet 2. To be honest, we don't really know.

Treelet 1. We kind of know.

Amira.   What do you "kind of" know?

Treelet 2. There was another girl. Sorta like you.

Treelet 1. She didn't have green hair, though.

Amira.   Okay.

Treelet 2. He left her. Right here. Just like you.

Treelet 1. We got all up in his face.

Amira.   Guys. C'mon.

Treelet 2. He didn't say much. Just that...

Treelet 1. He's a Straddler. Supposed to be a secret.

Amira.   Who was the girl?

Treelet 2.   No idea. He said she wasn't ready either.

Treelet 1.   Said he's a "helper." It's his "job."

Treelet 2.   Something about "Transformation. Change."

Treelet 1.   Said he wasn't allowed to.

Amira.   "Allowed to" what?

Treelet 1.   Change. Said he's "stuck in-between."

Treelet 2.   Seemed pretty bummed about it.

Treelet 1.   Seemed super shady if you ask me.

Treelet 2.   Wait. Where are you going?

Amira storms up the same path she chose earlier. She's tired of being played for a fool. She's going to find this zipe-off and give him a piece of her mind. Anyone could have guessed the things he knew about her. Anyone with a vest could easily... Amira feels faint again. She steadies herself against the largest tree she can find. Her body is molten. Sweat drips from every pore. She remembers the last time she steadied herself on a tree. A large Douglas fir in front of the No Vest Bar. She remembers how naked she felt when she first took off her vest. She wonders if this will help now. Allow her body to cool down. Allow her chest and back to breathe. She glances about the empty forest and instantly feels silly for thinking anyone cares. She slips one arm out. Then the other. Careful to steady herself on the tree as she goes. It's off. The vest is off. She feels better. Naked. But better. She lays her vest across a low-hanging branch. She notices the vest appears happy sprawled out on the soft, fleshy-green needles. Amira remembers Mazz saying the vest is made of cotton-water. An amalgam of cotton and rainwater. She wonders if the vest feels more at home on the tree than it does on her. She also wonders if the tree will suddenly have access to the Collective. She laughs out loud. "Why would a tree want access to the Collective?" A crack of thunder interrupts the folly. "Thunder is always a reminder of how unimportant we are." Amira thinks. Rain floods the sky. Amira ducks into the giant split at the base of an enormous western red cedar. "It's like a cave." She says out loud. Her first thought inside the cave is this: "The smell inside here would be a good choice for a Starbucks aroma." Ice cold drops of rain are somehow still finding the top of Amira's neon celery hair. She looks up to see bits of a charcoal and marshmallow sky peeking through a rotted gap at the top of the tree's makeshift cave. Robust cedar branches frame the view. One solitary, icy raindrop, lands perfectly into Amira's left eye. She wonders if this is payback for thinking about Starbucks. Her leg is starting to feel weird again. Pain, but not bad pain. Really weird pain. This is the first time she's felt this for a while. She decides to leave the cozy tree cave and walk until the weirdness subsides. She's suddenly feeling less furious. Less vengeful. But still intent on finding that stupid old man. Give him a piece of her mind. The rain is letting up. Amira doesn't really mind the rain. Kind of loves it. "It was the thunder that made me run for cover."

Amira is fully aware that she has no idea where she's going. Up the big trail. Down through the hollow by the creek. Her leg is acting up. Is this where she was? Another big trail. Then another. Is this right? Down the steep ravine. Along the wet gully. Leg convulsing. So weird. Feels like stuff is actually moving inside it. Amira stops near the creek. Kneels down and cups her hands. The cold water flows around her hands so effortlessly. She wants a drink. But is mesmerized by the tactile sensations of the moment. Look at all the rocks on the bottom. Sulfur yellows. Brilliant oranges. Impossible reds. Infinite blacks. All exploding in a swirly, blurred mosaic created by the water's rushing surface. Listen. Just listen. The click-click-clicks of dozens of hidden red-legged frogs. The searching plea of a screech owl. Intricate high-pitched jazz solos from contented pacific wrens. Wafts of cold, wet air kissing her cheeks, lips, eyes, forehead. Reassuring scents from budding florets of organic life, dancing with decay. Beautiful detritus. Fueling more life. Amira scoops cold water into her pale, soft palms. And drinks. Water dribbles down her untouched wrists and forearms. Trickles down her untouched chin. Untouched neck. A single curious drop finds its way under her purple top. Sneaks down onto her untouched chest. Pauses on her untouched heart.

Old tree.   Good. Right?

Amira.   Wha -

Old tree.   The water. It's good. Right?

Amira.   I'm jus... I....um... wait...

Old tree.   Excuse me?

Amira.   You startled me. Wait a sec.

Old tree.   Oh.

Amira.   Can't a person get some privacy?

Old tree.   No offense?

Amira.   Yeah?

Old tree.   This is my home. I live here.

Amira.   Oh. Okay. Right.

Old tree.   Yeah.

Amira.   Sorry. I just...

Old tree.   That's okay. Most people don't get it.

Amira.   Yeah.

Old tree.   I don't take water from your home.

Amira.   I get it.

Old tree.   Most people don't get it.

Amira.   I do.

Old tree.   Do you? 'Cause it seems like you didn't.

Amira.   Wow.

Old tree.   What?

Amira.   Are there any nice trees?

Old tree.   What's that mean?

Amira.   I dunno. Every tree I meet, seems...

Old tree.   Angry?

Amira.   No. Not Angry. Just...

Old tree.   Miffed?

Amira.   No.

Old tree.   Grumpy? Frustrated?

Amira.   No. No. Just a little - vacuous.

Old tree.   So you think I'm - whatever that word was?

Amira.   Vacuous?

Old tree.   Yeah. You think I'm vabulous?

Amira.   Vacuous.

Old tree.   Vabulous.

Amira.   Vacuous.

Old tree.   That's what I said.

Amira.   You said vabulous.

Old tree.   Don't make fun of my lisp.

Amira.   Sorry.

Old tree.   The smartest trees don't live here.

Amira.   Oh. Wow. Where do they live?

Old tree.   Far away.

Amira.   How far?

Old tree.   As far away from people as they can get.

Amira.   They don't like people?

Old tree.   No. I mean. Some do. But...

Amira.   But what?

Old tree.   Um.

Amira.   What?

Old tree.   Nothing. I've said enough.

Amira.   Where would I go to find them?

Old tree.   Ha. There's only one place.

Amira.   Where's that?

Old tree.   I can't tell you.

Amira.   Why not?

Old tree.   It's a secret.

Amira.   Who says?

Old tree.   I can't tell you.

Amira.   Can you give me a hint?

Old tree.   I already have.

Amira.   That it's far away?

Old tree.   Yes.

Amira.   Where people don't go.

Old tree.   Yes.

Amira.   That could be anywhere.

Old tree.   Look. I've already told you too much.

Amira.   Have you been there?

Old tree.   Of course not.

Amira.   Why not?

Old tree.   Look. Do you want more water?

Amira.   No.

Old tree.   Fine. I'm going back to sleep.

Amira.   Okay.

Old tree.   Good. Fine.

Amira.   Fine.

Honestly? The old tree doesn't really seem to want to go to sleep. It's just a line. Amira knows this. But she also knows asking for privacy is always tricky. So she doesn't push. She walks back up the hillside trail. Both legs are pulsing. "Oh no. Wait a sec. The other leg, too? No way. Maybe I'm just imagining it. Maybe it's because I knelt down by the creek for so long. Wow. This feels really weird. Why does it feel like stuff is moving inside?"

It's getting dark. Amira knows she should head home. But she keeps walking. She wonders how long it takes to get somewhere when you don't know where you're going. This makes her giggle. She wonders if the smartest trees giggle. She wonders who decided those particular trees are the smartest trees. It's getting cold. Colder than she's admitting. Then it hits her. She doesn't have her vest. Panic shatters the brief calm. Amira frisks her body. "Where is it? The creek? The gully? On the hillside? No wonder my legs feel weird. No wonder I'm lost. No wonder I don't know what to do. How can I remember where my vest is, if I can't use my vest to remember? I'm nothing without my vest. Nothing! Wait, Amira. Stay calm. Stay calm. Breathe, Amira. Just breathe."

A medium-sized black cottonwood tree, in the final

throes of life, cracked and ravaged with decay, watches as
Amira fails to collect herself.

Dying tree. You're okay.
Amira.   No.
Dying tree. Yes you are.
Amira.   I lost my vest.
Dying tree. You're fine.
Amira.   My legs feel really weird. I'm cold. I'm lost.
Dying tree. You're okay.
Amira.   I'm not okay.
Dying tree. Yes you are. Better shape than me.
Amira.   What's wrong with you?
Dying tree. I'm dying.
Amira.   Yeah, well. Trees die.
Dying tree. Ouch.
Amira.   Sorry. I'm just scared.
Dying tree. I know.
Amira.   Are you sick?
Dying tree. More dying, than sick.
Amira.   Can I help?
Dying tree. Do you mean it?
Amira.   Sure. What can I do?
Dying tree. Would you replant me?
Amira.   What? Replant you? Really?
Dying tree. Not here. Near the smarter trees.

Amira.   Again with the smart trees.

Dying tree.   You've heard of them?

Amira.   Sort of.

Dying tree.   Would you take me there?

Amira.   Look. I want to help. But I can't carry you.

Dying tree.   No carrying. Take a cutting.

Amira.   Cutting?

Dying tree.   Just cut off a few of my growth tips.

Amira.   They all look dead.

Dying tree.   Thanks.

Amira.   Sorry. Like these?

Dying tree.   Wait-wait-wait. Yes. But not yet. You need soil.

Amira.   Like, from here? By your trunk?

Dying tree.   No, no. This soil is the reason I'm dying.

Amira.   Oh.

Dying tree.   We need alluvial soil. Loose soil.

Amira.   Like, from over there?

Dying tree.   From a creek bank. Sandy soil. No big rocks.

Amira.   I'd have to go back to the creek.

Dying tree.   Okay.

Amira.   Um. I'm really cold. And it's getting dark.

Dying tree.   Ah. Okay. Got it. Thanks anyway.

Amira.   No no. What about tomorrow?

Dying tree.   Tomorrow?

Amira.   Yeah. I could come in the morning.

Dying tree. I can't ask you to do that.

Amira.   You've already asked me a lot.

Dying tree. True.

Amira.   I can bring supplies. Food. Camping stuff.

Dying tree. I don't really need anything.

Amira.   Not for you. For me.

Dying tree. Ah, yes. Right.

Amira.   How long does it take to walk to the smarter trees?

Dying tree. I don't walk. So...

Amira.   Can you guess?

Dying tree. Um. Three days?

Amira.   Makes sense. Far enough to avoid people.

Dying tree. How'd you know the smarter trees avoid people?

Amira.   Just a guess.

Dying tree. Hmm.

Amira.   Well...

Dying tree. I like your green hair.

Amira.   Thanks.

Dying tree. See you tomorrow then?

Amira.   If I can find you.

Dying tree. You'll find me.

Amira.   Can I ask you something?

Dying tree. Of course.

Amira.   How am I able to talk to you without...

Dying tree. Without wearing your treephones?

Amira.   Yeah.

Dying tree. It's a gift. Pretty rare.

Amira.   Not sure I like it.

Dying tree. You don't have a choice.

Amira.   Sorry?

Dying tree. It's who you are.

Amira.   What does that mean?

Dying tree. Treephones were made to "listen" to trees.

Amira.   Yeah?

Dying tree. One-way communication only.

Amira.   I know. Trees do the talking. People listen.

Dying tree. Right. But people talking to trees?

Amira.   Yeah?

Dying tree. I've never met anyone who could do this.

Amira.   So I'm a freak.

Dying tree. No way. You kidding?

Amira.   If it's so rare, then I'm a freak.

Dying tree. Not true.

Amira.   I've always been a freak.

Dying tree. You have a gift.

Amira.   I don't want a gift. I want, I want...

Dying tree. What do you want?

Amira.   I dunno. No idea what I want anymore.

Dying tree. Welcome to the universe.

Amira.   What's that supposed to mean?

Dying tree.   Wanting creates confusion.

Amira.   Wait. You "want." You want me to move you.

Dying tree.   True.

Amira.   So. Are you confused?

Dying tree.   Wanting to live in better soil isn't confusing.

Amira.   You also want to move near the smarter trees.

Dying tree.   Yep. Wow. Got me. There's the confusion.

Amira.   Look. I gotta go. It's almost dark.

Dying tree.   Okay.

Amira.   If I can find you, I'll see you tomorrow.

Dying tree.   You'll find me.

Amira.   Doubt it.

Dying tree.   That's the spirit.

Amira.   Heh.

Amira walks back up the hillside trail. Past the creeks. Over the small ridge. She's a long way from home. But somehow, she's finding her way. Just walk. Don't think. Hey. Look at that. It's not so dark outside the forest. Not nearly as late as she thought. Her legs are feeling less weird. Amira crests the last treeless bluff and digests the delicate lights of Nowhood beginning to take hold. Amira prefers a comfortable distance when thinking about the people of Nowhood. "They're all right down there." She thinks. "Doing what people do, I guess. Ignorant of their own possibilities. Swimming through gelatinous lagoons of sameness. Content without love in their comfy, finite ecosystem." Amira knows she's part of the same ecosystem. Equally ignorant of her own possibilities. She walks along the edge of the marsh to her comfy hole. Determined to head out in the morning with an astutely-organized backpack stuffed with supplies. She likes the thought of having supplies. Taking only what one truly needs. And for the first time, Amira realizes something about herself she never thought she'd think. She likes not wearing a vest.

A long time ago, Henry and Natalie made a pact. Just once, see if they could both make it to the Work is Work warehouse before the sun comes up. No reason. Just to see if they could do it. Today is the magic day. Now that they did it? They're not sure what to do. There's barely enough light to see each other sitting in the circle of plastic green chairs.

Henry.	Any word from Amira?
Natalie.	Nope.
Henry.	I get a weird feeling.
Natalie.	Like?
Henry.	I dunno.
Natalie.	Use your words, Henry.
Henry.	Like she's not coming back.
Natalie.	Can you blame her?
Henry.	I know, but.
Natalie.	None of us really want to be here.

Henry.   Yeah. But I like the idea of tricking myself.

Natalie.   Tricking yourself into being here?

Henry.   No. Tricking myself into wanting.

Natalie.   Ah. Yep.

Henry.   Do we have any clients today?

Natalie.   Nope. None.

Henry.   Tomorrow?

Natalie.   Nope. Just waiting for walk-ins.

Henry.   What are we doing?

Natalie.   Well. Um.

Henry.   I mean, seriously? What are we doing?

Natalie.   Well. I sell Happy water.

Henry.   Yeah. I have a drive-thru therapy business.

Natalie.   And?

Henry.   Why don't we leave?

Natalie.   For good?

Henry.   Maybe.

Natalie.   Wow. Do we need to do anything?

Henry.   We could put up a sign.

Natalie.   Do we need a sign?

Henry.   Seems like the gracious thing to do.

Natalie.   What do we put on the sign?

Henry.   I dunno. Words.

Natalie.   I'll get paint.

Henry.   I'll think up words.

And just like that. The Work is Work warehouse is closed for business. No one expected this. Yet no one will be confused or surprised. People in Nowhood. People everywhere, actually. Are always okay with everything.

Amira wakes with purpose. She spent the entire night packing. Sleeping just long enough to know she slept. Amira gallops up the hillside trail in the morning fog. Her amaranth colored backpack overstuffed with supplies and a secret. A secret no one can know. She also has some of those dehydrated meal packets that fit in your pocket. Supposedly, these packets offer the same FoodMachine deliciousness, one boiling cup of water away. The sun peeks through the grey mist. Amira closes her eyes and positions her face into the warm light. It feels better than warm light. It feels like nourishment. With her eyes closed, she hears the sharp, nasty chatter of a Steller's Jay. She wonders if the Steller's Jay feels threatened by her enormous pink backpack. Amira's eyes gently disappear into a giant smile.

Amira walks like a woman unfamiliar with carrying a heavy backpack. Which is exactly what she is. She remembers when she first bought this backpack. She was supposed to go on a trip with Natalie to help bottle the first samples of Happy water. Natalie's initial plan was to capture rainwater far away from Nowhood. Then she realized rainwater is now the same everywhere. One of the unforeseen advantages of having conquered pollution. Natalie started bottling Happy right outside her grey hole in Nowhood. She decided to add a "single tear of joy" at the very last moment. Just as a point of differentiation. It worked. Natalie is well on her way to buying back most of North America. Returning the land back to the spirits of her ancestors. Amira crests the ridgeline and dips into the forest. Amira briefly wonders about the irony of Natalie's accomplishments. "She worked her whole life to return stolen property. Only to realize there's no one left to return it to. What if Natalie never existed? What would have happened to all that stolen land? Would I be the same person I am today if I'd never met Natalie?" These are tricky questions. So she keeps on walking. Secretly delighted she finally has a worthy purpose for her giant, bright pink backpack. The trail ascends and descends into familiar rhythms. Amira realizes she actually knows where she is. "How can you know something without knowing anything?" Amira thinks. Yesterday, she doubted she'd find her way back. Yesterday's worry has given light to today's purpose. The purpose of helping a sick friend. Hey. Her legs don't feel weird. Not even a little bit. And her once labored stride is surprisingly strong under the weight of the giant bright pink supply ship floating on her back. As she navigates the last hillside, she sees her friend. Amira's heart unexpectedly flutters with joy. She literally skips toward the tree.

Amira.   Hey! I made it.

Dying tree.

Amira.   It was easy to find you. Just like you said.

Dying tree.

Amira.   I brought scissors. And some plastic cups.

Dying tree.

Amira.   Figured I'd put your cuttings in plastic cups.

Dying tree.

Amira.   Easier to carry them that way.

Dying tree.

Amira.   How are you doing? Oh. And please...

Dying tree.

Amira.   Do not make fun of my giant pink backpack.

Dying tree.

Amira.   Where do I get the soil again? By the creek?

Dying tree.

Amira.   Hello?

Dying tree.

Amira.   Are you resting? Hello??

Dying tree.

Amira.   Are you...

Dying tree.

Amira.   No.

Dying tree.

Amira.   No-no-no.

Amira rips through her backpack, fumbling for her treep-hones. Suddenly, everything she packed seems useless. Dozens of pairs of colorful socks. Multiple grey knit hats with fuzzy balls on top. A glass flute she's never played. A piece of driftwood that looks like a bird. Wait. There. At the bottom. Cold and icy blue. Her treephones. She grabs them both and violently jams them into each ear.

Amira.   Hello?

Dying tree.

Amira.   Hello? Are you there?

Dying tree.

Amira.   Can you hear me?

Dying tree.

Amira.   Please tell me you can hear me.

Dying tree.

Amira.   Please?

Dying tree.

Amira.   Say something.

Dying tree.

Amira.   Please.

Dying tree.

Amira.   Anything.

Dying tree.

Amira.   Please?

Dying tree.

Amira.

Dying tree.

Amira.

Dying tree.

Amira drops to her knees. Looks up into the decayed limbs of her friend. And openly weeps into a pile of colorful socks and grey knit hats. She cries like she's never cried before. Allowing every inch of her pain to be expressed and accounted for. "Is this normal? Am I okay? All this because of a silly tree?" Suddenly, Amira wants to sleep. She wasn't sleepy a minute ago. She grabs all her colorful socks and hats. Balls them into a pillow. Hugs her pink backpack. Lies down like an invisible embryo. And closes her drowning eyes.

Amira dreams a different dream. She's not in a meadow. Nor on a hillside. Amira knows she's not outside at all. She's naked and floating. Curled up inside a glass cylinder filled with clear fluid. She feels old and full of wisdom. But her yet unformed body says otherwise. She can hear people talking. Nothing of consequence. Work babble. Crass judgements about coworkers punctuated with chirps of counterfeit laughter. She is unnoticed and safe. Yet lonely. She awakens to the reassuring shrill of pacific wrens.

Amira keeps her head down until her eyes adjust. She knows exactly where she is. She knows her friend is dead. She knows she didn't sleep long. She collects her makeshift pillow garments and stuffs them into her pink backpack. She removes the treephones from her ears. Grabs the plastic cups. And heads to the creek where the soil is exactly what the dying tree was describing. Sandy soil. Alluvial soil. Creek bank soil. No rocks. She scoops the damp earth into three plastic cups. Walks quickly back to her dead friend. Takes the scissors out of her backpack. Delicately cuts off three nubile branch tips. Plunges her index finger into the soil. And places the new cuttings into the cups. She packs the earth around the cuttings firmly. Careful not to break the fragile stems. As she stops to admire her work, a curious pacific wren lands on her forearm. Without moving a muscle, she watches the bird rotate its tiny head to examine her up close. Amira smiles her tiniest smile. "A big smile might startle her." Amira isn't sure how she knows it's a female. She just knows. When the wren eventually flies off, Amira feels a tornado of warmth whirl through her body.

The trail is no longer clear and obvious. But the sky is exactly this. Clouds do not exist. At least for the moment. Amira hoists her bright pink backpack and slings it across her shoulders with purpose. The three earthen cups secured at the top with straps improvised from colorful socks. It's warm above the treetops. This is an educated guess. Warmer than yesterday. The air in the forest is calm and cool today. Not nearly as cold as yesterday.

Amira has no idea where's she's headed. But she's trusting her instincts. Trusting her instincts is something Amira never thought she'd do. Not wearing a vest, she only knows she needs to keep walking. "Walk for about three days." She silently repeats to herself. "Until all signs of people disappear."

The thimbleberry plants have begun to disappear. The trails were once lined with them. Amira wonders if the raspberry-looking fruits are safe to eat. They almost look too good. Early blackberries in Nowhood look delicious. Purple and plump. Only to explode into a bomb of acrid and sour. "This must be a way for plants to discourage creatures from early snacking." Amira thinks. "Until all the berries get a chance to mature."

An occasional woodpecker appears by sound only. Always high in the treetops. She suspects it's a Pileated Woodpecker. With the bright red hat. It's not really a hat. It's a crest. But Amira likes to think unusually colorful accents in nature are a "consciously-conspicuous personal choice." The sound is alarmingly sharp and crisp. A knocking not unlike the violent rat-tat-tat of a knuckle on a Starbucks bathroom door. Amira would like to think of another way to describe this sound. But it's not happening.

Amira remembers sitting at the No Vest Bar. She remembers Krop. She remembers Henry insisting she go there. She remembers lots of things. Puddles of fresh rain in the streets of Nowhood innocently reflecting the beautiful sky. Making it impossible for one to ever forget to look up. She remembers the gentle and incisive intelligence of Natalie. How Natalie's longing for deeper spiritual connection always seemed to be hiding behind a veil of regret. She remembers Mazz in the Vesteteria. So genuinely happy to offer Amira a comfortable new vest for insisting on the death of the name Sleeveless Wonders. She remembers the young children walking together in straight lines on the sidewalks. Holding each other's tiny hands. Wondering if any of them retain memories of their tranquil gestation inside silent clear silos. She thinks about the Swish. The train powered by a sea of unknown legs. She thinks about the deer. The deer who somehow worked their way into people's holes and hearts. And yes, their beds. She thinks about Janet. Her nefarious partner in crime with impromptu hopes of finding a date. A rapacious Saheed running loose in an era not his own. She reflects on the disparate collection of people she's given advice to at the Work is Work warehouse. The well-meaning small talk from Sparks at the FoodMachine. She thinks about those terrible fortune cookies with the wonderfully obtuse fortunes. And those delightful, habit-forming, plastic-wrapped globs of spontaneously-created sustenance. Glorious, predictable, completely unrecognizable, "food."

Amira suddenly realizes she hasn't eaten. And it's getting dark. She looks around for a nice flat place to camp. There's a good spot. Hey. There's another one. "Too many choices." Amira thinks. The forest spends its whole life creating a soft, pillowy floor. But no one stays long enough to notice.

Above the treetops, the night sky is already purple. Every bird in the forest is singing. Chattering away in a symphony of existential delight. Amira pours hot water into the pocket-sized cylinder of FoodMachine powder. This particular one is labeled "Raisin Potato Mash." "Sounds like a meal that might taste better eaten outside." Amira thinks. Now Amira has her doubts. "It smells like deer food." Amira thinks. Amira has no idea what deer food smells like. But she's smart enough to guess. She gently squeezes a tiny bit into her mouth. "Hmm. Wow. Tastes like... like... deer food." Every flavor, literally, cancels the others out. Salty cancels sweet. Bland cancels spicy. Starchy cancels fresh. Amira thinks a better name for this lovely dehydrated meal packet would be "Grey Blah." Despite these revelations? She eats every last bit. "One can't be picky when the body needs fuel."

Amira snuggles into her sleeping sack. She's been dying to try it out. It was the most expensive thing on her list when she went shopping with Natalie. Natalie made it clear that a good night's sleep was absolutely the most important thing when camping. "Sleep is your reward for a hard day's work." Amira can still perfectly remember the sagacious look in Natalie's eyes when she said it.

Amira feels deep inside her hip pocket for her treephones. Maybe she'll listen to some trees before she drifts off to sleep. She wonders why she hasn't been able to hear any trees talking without wearing them. "Maybe they're all startled by my giant pink backpack." She thinks. As she nestles the warm, bright-blue-glass orbs into her cold ears, she hears a reassuring chorus of treelet conversation.

Treelet 1.   What if we invented a new word for it?

Treelet 2.   New word? For what?

Treelet 3.   For 'night.' When there's no moon.

Treelet 2.   We can't do that.

Treelet 1.   Sure we can.

Treelet 3.   What about bleam? Or vixalon?

Treelet 1.   I like bleam.

Treelet 3.   Yeah.

Treelet 2.   Have a nice 'bleam.'

Treelet 3.   See you in the morning. 'Goodbleam.'

Treelet 1.   Hahaha.

Treelet 2.   Hahaha.

Amira removes her treephones and wriggles them back into her warm hip pocket. She gazes one last time into the night sky. It's as clear as she's ever seen it. White neon stars atop thick black velvet. Amira notices she's rubbing her feet together at the bottom of her sleeping sack. Each foot attentively caressing the other. "Two good friends, these feet."

This is Amira's last thought before she closes her eyes.

As Amira sleeps, Nowhood is about to experience a loss. The professional sports team so many lustfully follow, the Nowhood Fallers, is about to release a public statement that they are moving to a previous era. Here is the official release: "Dear people of Nowhood. The Green era has nothing left to offer us. We have unanimously decided to return to the Yellow Era where we will attempt to dominate the earliest days of the Professional Falling League. This should help foster a more competitive environment in subsequent eras." This unexpected news will likely hit many in Nowhood extremely hard, forcing some diehard fans to reexamine their priorities. Sales of oranges may also plummet.

Amira wakes to the same symphony of birds as the night before. But the songs are more subdued. More space between the notes. Amira wonders if this is a conscious effort. An unwritten respect for the gradual appearance of a new day. Amira inspects the three earthen cups. The makeshift berm she created in the forest detritus appears to have done its job. The cuttings look pretty good. If not a little dry. She dribbles water onto her fingers mimicking the act of rain falling from the forest canopy. She secures the three cups to the top of her backpack. Hoists the bright pink monstrosity over her shoulders. And struts confidently into the unknown.

Back in Nowhood, life resumes without incident. When

the deepest questions revolve around sports teams or pet deer, things stay cozy. People seem genuinely pacified by the absence of choice.

Janet is crazy-busy as usual. She's always busy. When you put the words "Ten Seconds" in the name of your business? You'd better be prepared to deliver. Janet tends to see lots of repeat customers. She chooses not to acknowledge them. They, in turn, choose to pretend they've never been to Ten Second Dating Yoga. But something is very different today. She notices a man she's certain has never been here before. Yet? She absolutely *knows* him. No way. No boochin' way. It's the Visitor. It's Saheed.

Janet.	Where's Amira?
Saheed.	Who?
Janet.	The woman you're supposed to be with.
Saheed.	No clue. I bailed out.
Janet.	What?
Saheed.	I jumped out of the car. Chick was whack.
Janet.	You did what?
Saheed.	Both you guys are whack.
Janet.	Listen to me.
Saheed.	Let go of my thro-a-t...
Janet.	You tell me where she is, understand?
Saheed.	I - I - don't - know - I -
Janet.	You and I are taking a little trip.

Saheed.   Wha - ?

Janet.   Back to the Transfer Dome.

Janet was once a deer masseuse. She won't admit this. She likes to pretend it never happened. But it's true. Janet had a brief and highly unsuccessful career massaging people's pet deer. Not only are Janet's hands remarkably strong, they're dangerous. She (accidentally) learned how to grab deer by the brachial plexus, rendering them completely immobilized. Later, she found it works similarly, with men. Saheed is going back to the year 2350. Whether he likes it or not.

Back in the deeper recesses of the forest, Amira is making good time. She's beginning to wonder if she's going too fast. The dying tree guessed it would take three days. Amira wonders if she planted the cuttings correctly. She tries to imagine the science behind growing new trees from cuttings. It clogs up her brain. So she opts to dwell on things she understands: The soft carpet of decomposing leaves and needles cushioning her every step. The dancing, filtered light through the forest canopy. The cool, crisp air. The sounds. These beautiful sounds. Creatures hidden from view. Yet always respecting the aural capacity of their own arboreous theater. Amira wonders if the reason she's not hearing anything from the trees without her treephones is because she's losing her "gift." Maybe the gift was temporary. Ephemeral. Maybe she wasn't worthy of the gift. Maybe this gift is like the wind.

Traveling with no end. And no beginning. Maybe the gift has simply moved on. Maybe the gift found her boring. Or ugly. She's thinking a lot about the gift. Until she realizes, there is no gift. There is only Amira. Amira walking through a forest. Amira determined to fulfill the wishes of a dying tree. And for now, this is enough.

After stopping for lunch and taking a brief nap, Amira expertly hoists the huge pink backpack onto her shoulders. She's getting better at it. She used to dread lifting it onto her back. Now she kind of enjoys it. She can tell she's getting stronger. The cuttings seem to enjoy the short breaks. She likes setting them down on the forest floor beside her while she eats or rests. She particularly enjoys the act of repeatedly securing the cuttings onto the top of her backpack. "I'm responsible for their safety." She thinks. As Amira gracefully struts up an unusually steep incline, she can feel something is different. Something is changing. It's not the light. Or the air. Not the challenge of the terrain. Wait. There. What is that? Something is moving. Dark and swift. Pausing. Then darting. Delicate licorice ferns jutting from the rocky wall are moving. Inconsistently. Unnaturally. Then? Nothing. Quiet. Weird quiet. Amira isn't moving. Her pounding heart the only audible sound. Then? Just like last time. A faint whiff of smoke. Rich. Colorful. Peat. Black cherry. She glances up slowly. There. On the branch. The same stupid

old man with a pipe. The same stupid smile on his stupid
bearded face.

Old man.   Hello.
Amira.   Really?
Old man.   You look angry.
Amira.   Just tell me what you want.
Old man.   I don't want anything.
Amira.   Can I go, then?
Old man.   Of course.
Amira.   Tell me how you knew everything.
Old man.   How I what?
Amira.   How you knew who I was.
Old man.   No idea what you're talking about.
Amira.   Oh please.
Old man.   Have we met?
Amira.   Will you stop? Please stop.
Old man.   I'm sorry.
Amira.   How did you know about the books?
Old man.   The what?
Amira.   The books. Under my bed.
Old man.   What's a "books?"
Amira.   Book.
Old man.   I don't know very much. I'm sorry.
Amira.   You knew about Janet. And the Visitor.
Old man.   What's a Janet?

Amira.	C'mon.
Old man.	Where are we going?
Amira.	Look. I'm going.
Old man.	Now I can't come?
Amira.	What?? No.
Old man.	You just invited me.
Amira.	No I didn't.
Old man.	Yes you did.
Amira.	No - I didn't.
Old man.	Did so.
Amira.	Did not.
Old man.	Fine. I didn't want to go anyway.
Amira.	Fine.
Old man.	Good.
Amira.	Good.
Old man.	Where are you going?
Amira.	Enough! Enough!! Okay? Enough.
Old man.	I like your green hair.
Amira.	Thanks. I'm going now.
Old man.	I also like the pink thing growing on your back.
Amira.	It's a backpack.
Old man.	Don't be embarrassed.
Amira.	What?
Old man.	I once had a pink thing growing on my chin.
Amira.	It's not growing.

Old man.   It'll probably fall off.

Amira.   Stop! I'm going now.

Old man.   You sure I can't come?

Amira.   Look. I'm leaving. Do *not* follow me.

Old man.   Okay.

Amira.   I'm serious.

Old man.   Okay.

Amira.   Stay there.

Old man.   Okay.

Amira.

Old man.   Bye.

Amira.

Old man.   Aren't you gonna say bye?

Amira.

Old man.

Amira.

Old man.   Can you still hear me?

Amira.

Old man.

Amira.

Old man.   I can still kind of see you.

Amira.

Old man.

Amira.

Old man.   I like your green hair, again.

Amira walks quickly and circuitously away. A straight line might give her destination away. Even if she doesn't really know where she's headed. What just happened? Is this real? Is she imagining things? Is she getting enough sleep? Is this a reaction from the Grey Blah meals she's eating? How could she meet the same man twice? And have two completely different experiences? It's getting dark. Amira wants to rest. But she also wants to create a comfortable distance from the crazy old man. Okay. Maybe he's not crazy. But still. The first old man was clearly a zipe-job. The second old man... Wait. They have to be the same person. Right? She continues weaving her way up through the tangled legs of the forest. She's tired. Every bit of walking she's done has been "up." Amira is trying to recall the last time she walked "down." Up. Up. Up. All day long. Eventually, there has to be some downhill. Right? She eyes a tiny clearing tucked inside the brambled ferns. Wait. Not again. Movement. Dark and swift. Are you kidding? She slowly glances up. Peers through the tree branches. Nothing. No stupid old man. There. Again. Movement. In a sea of shaded bracken ferns. Ah. Wow. Phew. Two deer. Looking straight at her. Locked in a cautious stare. Amira smiles and lets out a giant breath of imprisoned air. I'm safe. The deer are safe. The deer will alert me if anyone approaches. "This must be where they sleep." Amira thinks. She takes off her large pink backpack and makes camp. She's gotten so efficient setting up for the night, she doesn't even remember climbing into her sleeping sack. Wow. It's really dark. She can't see a single star. Maybe the clouds are too thick. She feels along the bumpy ground with her cold hand and shapes a berm beneath the shelter of the ferns. She nestles the tree cuttings in for the night. Amira consciously avoided making dinner. Why give away your location to a stupid bearded old man with the drifting scent of uninspiring food. As she closes her tired eyes, she begins to giggle. "I'm sleeping with deer." She rides the laughter into a welcomed night of quiet, blissful sleep.

The third day awakens with a crash of thunder. Amira opens her drenched eyes to a timely greeting from the thick morning clouds. A flash of panic. She forgot to water the cuttings last night. Ah. But the clouds had her back.

Amira surprises herself with how quickly she packs. It's becoming effortless. As she hoists the backpack onto her shoulders, she notices the tops of the heads of the two deer. They seem perfectly happy laying right there in the rain. Amira wonders if they have plans for the day. As she walks away, she wonders why deer would ever trade the tranquility of the forest for a "herd pod" in an urban hole.

The rain is letting up. The morning sun is making a feeble attempt to get noticed. Amira trods up the steep makeshift trail. Up. Always up. Where is the down? She knows this should be the day she reaches the smarter trees. She remembers how the first old tree near the creek referred to them as the "smartest trees." The dying tree simply called them "smarter" trees. She likes the idea of a group of *smarter* trees. "Smartest" just sounds elitist. She wonders if there are any smarter trees living by themselves. "Trees who prefer the sanctity and reflective solitude of their own company. Trees who don't need to belong to a group." She wonders if she's passed one of these trees already. "A quiet tree with enough wisdom to stay quiet. Hey. Look at that. There's a huge clearing ahead. Almost like a - "

That's when it happens. "Crack." Amira's leg slips into a hole the size of a bucket. As she falls forward, her leg stays put, snapping her leg like a branch. Everything inside the pink backpack is catapulted forward, vomiting its contents over Amira's head and over the edge of an enormous cliff. Everything disappears. The three cups of alluvial soil with the precious cuttings. The Grey Blah meals. The sleeping sack. The stupid glass flute. The piece of driftwood shaped like a bird. The treephones. The makeshift pillow garments. All her supplies. Everything except the secret hidden at the bottom of the pack. All forcefully catapulted into the depths of an unexpected forested canyon. Amira is in excruciating pain. Pain previously unimaginable to her. This is bad. And Amira knows it.

First things first. "Unbuckle the backpack waist-belt. There. Now slowly work the backpack around to your front. Careful. No pressure on the leg. Okay. Next? How do you remove your leg from the hole? Wait. Use your arms. Bend at the waist. Easy now. Slow. Ow. Ow. Ow. Tears drain from Amira's face. Crawl out on your belly, Amira. That's it. Claw at the ground. Use your nails. Claw and pull. Claw and pull. Stay low. Lower. Be a snake. Pull your body through the dirt. Claw and pull. That's it. Let the bright pink backpack help. Use it like a gurney. Little bits. Easy. Easy. Pull. Pull. Claw and pull. Little more. You're almost out. There. You're out. Now what? Rest. Ow. Ow. No. Um. Roll over? Onto your back? Why does that feel wrong? Just stay on your stomach for now. Breathe. Just breathe, Amira. Breathe through the pain. You got this."

Amira wonders if this might be the end. Her mind races through a furious blur of solutions and failures. Flashes of faces. Friends. Clients. Strangers. Flashes of home. Bed. Chair. Table. She knows the leg is bad. She wants to look. But doesn't. What can she do if the bone is poking out? She's days away from any help. She decides to look. Taking a deep breath, she grabs the base of some bracken ferns and rolls onto her side. "Ow. Ow. There. This is better already. Yes. Lying on your side helps. Okay. Now. Survey the leg. Slow, Amira. Don't be shocked. Just a glance. Look for blood, Amira. Red is easy to see. Hey. *Hey.* No red. Nothing.

Examine closer. Wait...What's poking out? Reach down and feel it, Amira. Touch it. There...What? No. Can't be. But it is. A stick. A thick, broken, damp, wooden stick. Sticking out of my leg. What the... Did it stab through my pants when I fell? Wait. No blood. Maybe I got lucky. Maybe the stick is acting like a cork. Holding the blood in."

The gorge was unexpected. But it shouldn't have been. Amira knows enough about terrain to know if you keep going up, eventually you'll be going down. She simply didn't expect the down part - to be a cliff. She feels extremely lucky she didn't fall into the gorge. She crawls on her belly to peer over the edge. Maybe it's not too deep. Wrong. The depth of the gorge startles Amira. She is literally, above everything. Even the birds. She looks down on an osprey gliding along in search of a meal. The raptor has no idea Amira is watching from above. Amira knows an osprey means fish. And fish mean water. Sure enough. There's a stream running through the gorge. It looks so thin and tiny from up here. But at this height, it could be an enormous river. The pain is coming on stronger. Announcing its seriousness in ascending waves. Then. On a rock ledge below. There. Just out of reach. A flash of light. Right there. Something lodged in the spindly branches of a red-flowering currant. "No way. The stupid glass flute. Why couldn't it be something good?" As Amira sighs, she sees something else - barely hanging onto a branch.

A lone plastic cup. Flipped upside down. She can't see if the cutting is still inside. She rolls sideways. Flattening the ferns like a steamroller. She uses her entire body to feel for sticks, roots. Anything to use as a tool to reach the cup. Amira smiles as she rolls onto a long curved branch jabbing her in the back. She suddenly remembers Henry's meaningless words at the drive-thru therapy shack. *"Everything you need is always nearby."* She reaches beneath her back. Secures the large curved stick in her trembling hand. And rolls to the edge of the gorge. It's perfect. Like a stick you'd buy at a store, if stores sold sticks. There's even a cluster of broken twigs on the end, like a grabber. She reaches down and snags the plastic cup on her first try. Hand over hand, she slowly works the branch back up the face of the cliff. As it gets close enough to grab, she sees that the cutting is still there. Everything is intact. Even the alluvial soil. Clasping the cup with her shaky fingers, Amira begins to cry. She carefully sets the cutting down on the ground next to her cracked lips, dirty cheeks and bright green hair. Almost caressing the cup with her face. Amira closes her eyes. And weeps. Her tears, gently, lovingly, inadvertently, watering the cutting.

Amira isn't sleeping. Or dreaming. She is not in a meadow. Or stuck in a meeting. Amira is exactly where she is. Lying down on a precipice overlooking a gorge. She is fully aware of her tears. She is neither frightened nor sad. Restless nor calm.

She is exactly where she is. Exactly where she needs to be. She is completely immobilized, yet somehow? Inexplicably? Completely free. Trapped between the brutal reality of a raw human experience, and the transformative exhilaration of a pending metamorphosis. Amira has one goal. And one goal only. To plant this cutting near the smarter trees.

Amira opens her eyes. She knows time is a factor. Both for her. And the cutting. Amira methodically works her way to her knees using the branch as a crutch. The pain in her leg is intense. But she's not having it. Instead of ignoring it? She decides to talk to it.

Amira.	Proud of yourself?
Pain.	Excuse me?
Amira.	Proud of the work you're doing?
Pain.	I don't understand.
Amira.	I think you do.
Pain.	No. I mean. I've never talked to anyone.
Amira.	Oh.
Pain.	You're the first person who's ever reached out.
Amira.	Really?
Pain.	Yeah.
Amira.	Wow.
Pain.	I'm a little unprepared.
Amira.	I understand.
Pain.	Are you okay?

Amira.	I'm great. How are you?
Pain.	I'm okay.
Amira.	You sound defeated.
Pain.	Ha. You wish. I'm just not sure what to say.
Amira.	Ah.
Pain.	You gonna try to get your stuff?
Amira.	What stuff?
Pain.	Stuff that fell into the gorge.
Amira.	I got one of the cuttings.
Pain.	You don't care about anything else?
Amira.	No. The cutting is all that matters.
Pain.	So. Um. Can I have the glass flute?
Amira.	What? Oh. Sure.
Pain.	Wow. Thanks.
Amira.	You bet.
Pain.	I like your hair.
Amira.	Thanks.
Pain.	It's really green.
Amira.	Yep.
Pain.	Is it painful?
Amira.	No.
Pain.	Okay. Hmm.
Amira.	Yeah. Time to go.
Pain.	Okay. Bye.
Amira.	Bye.

Pain.	Wait. Amira?
Amira.	Yeah?
Pain.	Thanks for talking to me.
Amira.	Aw. You're welcome.
Pain.	No one ever does.
Amira.	Goodbye.
Pain.	Bye.

The same stick that helped Amira grab the cutting and get her to her feet, is now helping her walk. The entirety of Amira's weight is falling onto the trusty branch in measured, alternating steps. The pack is so much lighter now. But the irony of why, is not lost on Amira. She is, ever so slowly, limping down the same makeshift path she hiked up. The air is cool and strangely reassuring. The sun is playfully exploring gaps in the woods with its warm fingers. Amira knows she eventually needs to head left. Or right. She just doesn't know which. "As long as I'm not going backward." She thinks. "Or over the edge of another booching cliff." She rests every twenty or thirty arduous steps. Pain is very much a part of her world now. But the brief conversation she had with pain, helped. She wonders if conversation might be an undiscovered analgesic. Her labored pace is beginning to worry her. She's on her third day. In theory, she's already supposed to be arriving at the place where humans rarely go. The deepest part of the forest. Home of the smarter trees.

Amira decides to rest. Take off her pack. Lean on her walking branch. "At this speed," She thinks. "I'll never make it." It is precisely at this moment, Amira spies a fluorescent yellow banana slug slowly navigating its way across the damp organic undergrowth. The s-l-o-w-n-e-s-s is mesmerizing. The electric chartreuse slime, breathtaking. Amira suddenly feels guilty for not appreciating the relativity of her own gait. "To a slug? I'm traveling at light speed." Amira studies the banana slug's every movement. A deliberate sense of direction appears to be pouring out of this rubbery-wet, neon gastropod. Amira decides the banana slug is attempting to tell her which way to go. "Go left, Amira." She knows this is ridiculous. But she doesn't care. Amira is hungry for meaning outside the Collective. Left it is.

Amira painfully loads her nearly empty, electric pink backpack onto her shoulders. The remaining earthen cup and cutting, securely attached to the top of the pack near her left ear. Amira grasps her trusty walking branch, and limps off, at relative light speed, in the same direction as the banana slug.

All hints of a walking path, have disappeared. The going would be extremely measured and mechanical, even without this stupid leg thing. Waist high, wading awkwardly though a sea of pacific rhododendrons, evergreen huckleberry and lady ferns. Occasionally stung by the hypodermic leaves of a lone Oregon grape. All silently competing for territory under the shelter of the forest's protective umbrella.

Amira has been making her way downhill for most of the day. Barely perceptible. But the subtle drop in elevation is confirmed by a marked increase of tiny dendrite-like streams she's stepping through. They're almost like tiny springs. But Amira knows surface water when she sees it. It's trickling down from a higher source. Glacially working its way down-hill beneath an era's worth of organic debris. "Downhill is good." Amira thinks. She struggles to lower herself to dip her fingers in the trickle. She dribbles fresh water onto the cutting in the earthen cup riding up high next to her ear.

Amira smells fish. A sudden waft of briny decay kisses her nose and lips. As she pushes forward, it's becoming more pronounced. She stops. Holds perfectly still. Closes her eyes. And listens. There. Dry sticks breaking. Intermittent snaps. Close to the ground. Oh no. Getting closer. Amira bends forward at the waist, dipping her head. She can't lower her body any further with this leg. Oh god. So close. Heavy, clumsy, lumbering steps. A tree's length away. Then? Nothing. All movement. Sound. Everything. Stops. Amira stays bent over, hoping the cutting is okay. Maybe if she just stays like this. Maybe whatever it is, will think she's part of the forest. Maybe it can't even see her. Maybe it's just as frightened as she is. Maybe it's just a big deer.

Amira slowly raises her rigid body. As she straightens, a
thunderous, guttural snort interrupts all rational possibilities.
Towering above her on his powerful hind legs, stands a
mature black bear. Five or six Amira's worth. Teeth, claws,
muscle and bone. Amira can't run. Or fight. Or yell. Amira
stands there. Frozen. The bear speaks:

Bear.	You shouldn't be here.
Amira.	
Bear.	Got it?
Amira.	
Bear.	This is not your place.
Amira.	
Bear.	Hear me?
Amira.	
Bear.	You need to go.
Amira.	
Bear.	Go away.
Amira.	
Bear.	Look. I can eat you.
Amira.	
Bear.	If I hadn't just eaten, I probably would.
Amira.	
Bear.	
Amira.	Fish.
Bear.	

Amira.

Bear.   Yeah. How'd ya know?

Amira.

Bear.

Amira.   Smell.

Bear.

Amira.

Bear.   Aw. Yeah. Salmon. I didn't catch it, though.

Amira.

Bear.   Could have. I can catch salmon if I want.

Amira.

Bear.   It was laying on the ground.

Amira.

Bear.   Eagle probably dropped it.

Amira.

Bear.   Eagles think they're so cool.

Amira.

Bear.   You like eagles?

Amira.

Bear.   Well?

Amira.   I'm a little tense right now.

Bear.   Tense? Really? What's your name?

Amira.   Amira.

Bear.   Amira? Am I pronouncing that right?

Amira   Yes.

Bear.   So, Amira?

Amira.   Yes?

Bear.   You like eagles?

Amira.   Um. Yes. I think so.

Bear.   Know any?

Amira.   No.

Bear.   How do you know you like 'em then?

Amira.   Well. Um. They don't bother me.

Bear.   Yeah. Okay. They don't really bug me, either.

Amira.   Okay.

Bear.   They just think they're so cool, ya know?

Amira.   Okay.

Bear.   You still tense? You seem tense.

Amira.   A little.

Bear.   Can I ask what you're doing here?

Amira.   Just looking. Looking for a place.

Bear.   What place?

Amira.   Place a friend told me about.

Bear.   What's it called?

Amira.   I'm not sure.

Bear.   Who told you about it?

Amira.   Um. It's private.

Bear.   You on a quest?

Amira.   No. I mean. I don't know.

Bear.   You don't know where you're going?

Amira.   No.

Bear.   That's not weird to you?

Amira.   No. Why are you here? Where are you going?

Bear.   This is my job.

Amira.   What's your job?

Bear.   I can't tell you.

Amira.   Why not?

Bear.   It's private.

Amira.   Oh, okay.

Bear.   You said your stuff was private.

Amira.   Yeah. It is.

Bear.   See? Me, too.

Amira.   Okay.

Bear.   Okay.

Amira.   Alright then.

Bear.   Alright.

Amira.   Look. I need to get going.

Bear.   Okay, then. Go.

Amira.   Fine. I will.

Bear.   Fine.

Amira.   You gonna move?

Bear.   You wanna go this way? Past me?

Amira.   Yeah. That's the way I was going.

Bear.   Can't go this way.

Amira.   Why not?

Bear.   'Cause I said.

Amira.   Why not?

Bear.   Because you can't.

Amira.   Look. You don't own the forest.

Bear.   So?

Amira.   So either eat me. Or get out of the way.

Bear.   I told you, I already ate.

Amira.   I know. Salmon. I can still smell it. So move.

Bear.   Why do you need to go this way?

Amira.   Oh my god.

Bear.   What?

Amira.   You want to know where I'm going?

Bear.   Yeah.

Amira.   I'm going to the smarter trees.

Bear.

Amira.   I don't even know where they are.

Bear.

Amira.   I'm trying to plant a cutting from a dying tree.

Bear.

Amira.   He wanted to be near the smarter trees.

Bear.

Amira.   Where people don't go.

Bear.

Amira.   He's up here. On my shoulder. In the cup.

Bear.

Amira.   I don't even know if it's gonna work.

Bear.

Amira.   I've never done anything like this.

Bear.

Amira.   No idea where I'm headed.

Bear.

Amira.   No idea what I'm doing.

Bear.

Amira.   I don't even want to be here.

Bear.

Amira.

Bear.   Amira?

Amira.

Bear.   Are you crying?

Amira.   Of course I'm crying. I'm freezing. I have a stick poking out of my leg. I can't feel my hands or feet. I can't stop my body from shaking. I lost all my stuff over a stupid cliff. I'm out of food. I have no idea where I am. And now I'm clearly losing my mind because it actually seems like a stupid bear is harassing me and asking if I like eagles.

Bear.   Amira?

Amira.   What?

Bear.   Want to know what my job is?

Amira.   I don't care.

Bear.   I think you might.

Amira.   Doubt it.

Bear.   I'm a Sentry for the smarter trees.

Amira.   A what?

Bear.   A Sentry.

Amira.   What does that mean?

Bear.   I keep people away.

Amira.   Like me.

Bear.   Well.

Amira.   Well what?

Bear.   Depends.

Amira.   Depends on what?

Bear.   Two things.

Amira.   Okay.

Bear.   There are two kinds of people.

Amira.   Okay.

Bear.   Takers. And givers.

Amira.   Okay.

Bear.   Takers are strongly discouraged.

Amira.   So what am I?

Bear.   You tell me.

Amira.   I don't know.

Bear.   I think you do.

Amira.   I don't think I'm a taker.

Bear.   Okay.

Amira.   But I don't think I'm a giver, either.

Bear.   Really?

Amira.   Look. How can I know? It's impossible.

Bear.   No it's not.

Amira.   It's totally subjective. It's stupid.

Bear.   Amira. Answer one question.

Amira.   What?

Bear.   Why did you come here?

Amira.   I told you. I have no idea.

Bear.   Yes you do.

Amira.   I can't do this.

Bear.   Yes you can.

Amira.   Look. Just eat me or something?

Bear.   Amira. Listen to me.

Amira.   What?

Bear.   Why did you come here?

Amira.   I don't know, okay?

Bear.   Yes you do.

Amira.   I dunno. I guess...

Bear.   Yes?

Amira.   I came here...

Bear.   Yes?

Amira.   To plant this cutting.

Bear.   For yourself?

Amira.   No.

Bear.   Then you're a giver.

Amira.	That's it?
Bear.	Yep.
Amira.	So what's that mean?
Bear.	I'll walk you down.
Amira.	Where?
Bear.	To the smarter trees.

Amira's mind swirls in a sweaty fog. She is neither happy nor sad. Neither lost nor found. She only knows she's alive. Barely. And she wasn't eaten. Right now? These are the only two things that matter to her. She attempts to follow the bear through the brush. A clear path forged by his innocent, lumbering girth. The bear is intentionally slowing down to a snail's pace. Amira's pace. To say she is aware of what is happening right now would be inaccurate. Amira is barely here. Moving glacially on her last few molecules of fear. Fear is the only fuel she has left.

Bear.	Okay.
Amira.	Okay, what?
Bear.	This is it.
Amira.	We're here?
Bear.	No. This is where I leave you.
Amira.	Are we close?
Bear.	Kinda. Listen for water.
Amira.	Water?
Bear.	Yeah.

Amira.	Okay.
Bear.	Good luck.
Amira.	Um. Thanks.
Bear.	You bet.
Amira.	Really? That's it?
Bear.	That's it.
Amira.	Okay. Um...
Bear.	What?
Amira.	Nothing.
Bear.	You need a hug or something?
Amira.	No.
Bear.	Okay, then.
Amira.	Okay.
Bear.	Looks like you're dying.
Amira.	I am.
Bear.	Good sign.
Amira.	What?
Bear.	You'll see.
Amira.	What did you just say?
Bear.	Goodbye, Amira.

The bear adeptly spins his massive body on his front left paw and heads back the way they just came. Amira watches until the bear disappears completely from view. Until the bear is no longer sound or smell.

It's almost dark. Amira would like to pretend everything is

okay. But she can't. She's worse than ever. Her bad leg is now numb and worthless with a stick poking out of it. Her good leg is thumping in excruciating sympathy. If it wasn't for her trusty walking branch, she wouldn't be able to move.

Walking is not exactly what Amira is doing. It's more of an erratic lunge. A thrusting of her bulk, forward. Abusing the leg that still has feeling. Followed by a dramatic, full body-weight collapse onto the walking branch. This leaves the bad leg behind. The bad leg is then dragged along the ground like a dead body.

Amira is so cold. Yet somehow sweating like a swamp. She is profoundly thirsty. Painfully hungry. She imagines food as a bed. Water as a pillow. Yet the energy required to take a sip of water or tiniest bite of food, would end her. Every breath is shallow and contrived. Every pore, a geyser. She wants to stop. Right here. Right now. But she knows if she were to lie down this very second, she would never get up.

Amira is moving imperceptibly forward. Her failing, spent body serving now as a disconnected, reluctant mule. She still remembers the pace of the banana slug. She fails at an attempt to giggle in her mind. "The banana slug is the hare. I am the dead tortoise." Amira thinks.

It is precisely at this moment, she decides to lie down. "Just for a moment." She thinks. "A short rest. Rest is always good. Lie down, Amira. Lie down. For zipe sakes. Lie down." It doesn't even feel like her own voice. "Must be the voice of reason." She thinks.

Amira works her hands down the trunk of the walking branch. Hand over hand. Methodically desperate and woefully imprecise. Each grasp bearing the weight of the rest of her life. "The cool ground will help." She thinks. As she attempts to introduce her body to the forest floor, she collapses. The walking stick falling into the ferns like a dead tree. As she flies into unconsciousness, she hears a comforting sound. "Water. Just like the bear said." A stream. Fluttering. Playful. Liquid life. Bouncing innocently along agreeable rocks.

The forest dreams of Amira. The forest envisions her collapsing at its feet. The forest is always sleeping and always awake. Trees rarely dream together. For Amira, the forest is making an exception. Amira is oblivious to this collective dream. It is an invisible act of selflessness by the trees. Their dream is manifested as a single, communal question. No words are shared between the trees. Decisions are universally sculpted by the luminosity of feelings. And just like that. A decision has been reached.

Amira is being jostled about like a child in a coma. Eyes closed. Shivering violently. Freezing, yet burning up. A prisoner in a broken, dying body without choices. Amira is unable to summon the energy required to commit to consciousness. What she does not yet realize, is she is now being carried. Awkwardly cradled in the supporting arms of someone she has never met. Bucking up and down to the inconsistent rhythms of swift but oafish steps. It is the smell that ultimately begins to rouse Amira from her catatonic depths. Smoke. Rich and colorful. Familiar unapologetic breaths of black cherry and peat. Oh no. It can't be.

Old man.   You're heavier than I thought.

Amira.   What the... What are you doing?

Old man.   Carrying you.

Amira.   What? Stop. Put me down.

Old man.   Sorry. Can't.

Amira.   What? Let go of me. Put me down.

Old man.   We're almost there.

Amira.   Almost where?

Old man.   Place you were going.

Amira.   What? What are you talking about?

Old man.   Twenty more steps.

Amira.   Wait... where's the...

Old man.   Cutting? It's fine. It's with your pink luggage.

Amira.   Backpack.

Old man.   Packy pack.

Amira.   Backpack. Where is it?

Old man.   Already there. I took it first.

Amira.   Took it where?

Old man.   The place you were going.

Amira.   What is happening?

Old man.   Really? You don't know?

The old man gently sets Amira down on her useless legs. Amira briefly wakes to her own fragile reality. A fleeting, cascading narrative of failure. Amira holds onto the old man's shoulder as a crutch. He places the trusty walking branch in front of her. But she does not take it. Amira glances down. The bright pink backpack. The earthen cup and cutting. Both resting safely at her feet. She drips cold sweat on both like a stationary rain cloud. Amira is almost gone.

Old man.   Here. Drink this.

Amira.   No. What is it?

Old man.   A gift.

Amira.   I'm good.

Old man.   It's not a choice.

Amira.   I'm sorry?

Old man.   It's from the smarter trees.

Amira.   Why is the cup made of wood?

Old man.   Trees? Wood? Drink. There's no time.

Amira.   Eghh.

Old man.   Wow, you drink fast.

Amira: Awghh. Yuck.

Old man.   What's it taste like?

Amira.   It's terrible.

Old man.   I wouldn't know.

Amira.   Tastes like plastic.

Old man.   Really?

Amira.   Oh god. Oh god. No...no...

Old man.   What's wrong?

Amira.   Cake. I taste cake. Egghh...

Old man.   Wait. What are you doing?

Amira.   Trying to see what color it is.

Old man.   It's pretty. Like your hair.

Amira.   Oh god. It's green. It's the green drink.

Old man.   Right. That's the gift.

Amira.   I don't want it. I don't want a gift.

Old man.   What? Do you know how lucky you are?

Amira.   I don't want to be lucky.

Old man.   You've been chosen.

Amira.   I don't want to be chosen. I want to be left alone.

Old man.   Exactly. That's why you're here.

Amira.   What?

Old man.   You don't get it, do you?

Amira.   No.

Old man.   You're about to change.

Amira.   What?

Old man.   Your legs have already started. Can't you tell?

Amira.   A branch stabbed me.

Old man.   Hahaha. That's not a branch.

Amira.   What?

Old man.   That's a root. Your legs are becoming roots.

Amira.   No. Can't be.

Old man.   You're lucky. I wasn't allowed to change.

Amira.   What are you talking about?

Old man.   Not the whole way.

Amira.   Who are you?

Old man.   I'm a Straddler.

Amira.   What does that mean?

Old man.   I'm stuck in-between.

Amira.   I don't follow.

Old man.   Part human. Part tree.

Amira.   Um.

Old man.   More human than tree, really.

Amira.   I don't feel - well.

Old man.   That makes sense.

Amira.   I need to lie down.

Old man.   That makes sense, too.

Amira.   I'm going to bed now.

Old man.   Yep.

Amira.   Goodbye.

Old man.   Ha. You're funny.

Amira.   Take care of the books.

Old man.   Wait. What? I don't know what you just said.

Amira.   Protect the books. All nineteen.

Old man.   I'm sorry, I don't...

Amira.   Paper books. Bottom of my backpack.

Old man.   I didn't know there were any left.

Amira.   It's a secret.

Old man.   I love secrets. Anything else?

Amira.   The most important thing.

Old man.   Yes?

Amira.   Plant the cutting.

Old man.   Oh. Right. Of course. That's easy.

Amira.   Wait... Alluvial soil.

Old man.   Got it. Anywhere? Or?

Amira.   No. Listen to me. Please...

Old man.   I'm listening.

Amira.   Plant him...

Old man.   Yes?

Amira.   Near the smarter trees.

Old man.   Ha. That's easy.

Amira.   Why?

Old man.   We're already here.

Amira.   What?

Old man.   The smarter trees are all around us.

Amira.

Old man.   Amira?

Amira.

Old man.   You still with me?

Amira.

Old man.   Amira?

Amira.

Old Man.   Amira?

Amira.

Night takes gentle hold of the forest. Amira's eyes are closed with the same gentle grip. Amira is curled up like a deer on the soft detritus of the forest floor. Like a deer on a Herd Pod. This unexpected and untimely thought, encourages one last delicate smile to blossom on Amira's ravaged, unconscious lips. This is the very last thought Amira experiences before her very last breath. Amira is gone. Lying dead at the feet of the smarter trees. The place where humans rarely go.

The full arrival of darkness serves as a vast, empty stage for the unfolding first act. The forest, respectfully quiet just moments ago, is now uncharacteristically alive. Not with noise. Or chatter. On the contrary. There is a respectful, palpable, anticipatory hush. A calm, energized silence.

Amira is neither warm nor cold. The trees are neither awake nor asleep. The night sky is stuffed with clouds of charcoal and ripe plums. The necessary work is about to unfold.

The Straddler kneels.

Takes a deep breath.

He begins to cover Amira with soil and detritus. Starting at her feet, he meticulously covers every physical expression of Amira. Every bit of her changing legs. Forgotten ankles. Abused calves. Demolished shins. Tortured thighs. Anonymous hips. Abandoned stomach. All attentively blanketed with a conscious mixture of dark, silty loam. Consciously stirred together with select armfuls of sweet-smelling, decomposed organic debris.

An impromptu dance troupe of yellow warblers and violet-green swallows appear in the crisp, dark cerulean air. Darting. Swooping. Flashes of iridescent purples, yellows and neon green punctuate the sedulous work below. These birds should have traveled south long ago. It's unclear how much they know.

The Straddler slows down as he carefully conceals Amira's long, slender arms tucked comfortably against her chest. Now her tired shoulders. Delicate neck. The outermost wisps of Amira's neon green hair. The Straddler knows this should all be happening much quicker. But he chooses to adhere to the potent effects of grace and empathy.

The part he's been dreading comes now. He takes another deep breath. As he begins to reluctantly sprinkle handfuls of earth over Amira's beautiful face, he has an epiphany. The Straddler races off. As quickly as he leaves, he returns. An armload of soil overflowing his embrace. Not just any soil. Alluvial soil. From the banks of the nearby stream. The Straddler kneels and lovingly sifts the soil over Amira's peaceful face. Allowing it to lovingly caress her sleeping eyes, vulnerable cheeks and knowing lips.

He packs the soil firmly, deliberately, around her body. Using his spindly fingertips, he assures tactile soil contact with every exposed bit of Amira. As he finishes, he stands to admire his work. This is the first time he's ever performed this solemn duty. He suspects he did well.

The Straddler must now walk away. His work nearly done. But there are a few more important things he must tend to. He turns to look over his shoulder one last time. What looks like a fresh grave in the middle of the forest, is anything but. The Straddler is honored to be playing his part.

The deepest part of the night is about to unveil its gift. The sudden change in the air is obvious. No wind. No sound. A slow, steady rain begins to cascade from the fertile clouds above. The weight of the newly wet soil compressing Amira's dead body into the earth. As the first drops reach her skin, Amira begins to change.

Back in the slumbering town of Nowhood, innocuous events are unfolding simultaneously. Residents dream of things they already know. Quiet city trees prepare for another day. And perfect human embryos gestate in silent clear silos.

Henry is awake. As is Natalie. Along with Janet. Krop. Mazz. Dr. Velvy. Even Sparks. Normally, they all sleep like bricks. Except Sparks. Who spends the majority of his nights writing new lines for his fortune cookies. Even though none of these people are sleeping, they are all collectively dreaming of Amira. All fully awake. Fully conscious. Swimming with Amira in lakes they've never been to. Walking next to Amira along shorelines they don't recognize. Talking intimately with Amira about subjects they've never broached. And although no one has a clue what's happening in the deepest part of the forest right now, everyone who knows her, is bursting with Amira.

A fearless sun crests the Eastern horizon. The forest wakes to the breath of its own possibilities. Amira is still sleeping. But everyone around her is wide awake. Trees of all shapes and sizes buzzing like children waiting to unwrap presents. The morning's chorus of birds is deafening. The normal and subtle act of aural restraint is being willfully ignored. Even the nearby stream is bubbling with anticipation.

As the first kiss of sunlight finds Amira, she begins to wake. The light is intense. "The sun has a different feeling." Amira thinks. Sustenance over illumination. Amira deftly scans her memory for details of the previous night's events. She realizes there is a massive disconnect. Feelings of bottomless pain are gone. No more struggling for paltry breaths. No sense of pending cessation. Where there was desperation, there is calm. Where there was dread, there is possibility. As Amira opens her new eyes, she realizes things are very different. She is able to see, literally, everywhere. From the farthest mountain peaks licked with snow, to the nearby forests brimming with life.

She is able to see a migrating bevy of tundra swans navigate the highest atmospheric currents while simultaneously witnessing a pair of cinnamon teal land gracefully on a calm sapphire lake. She spies a red tree vole contentedly nibbling on the leaves of an indifferent Douglas fir while watching the distance lights of Nowhood click off to embrace the first hints of daylight. She can see the entire faint universe of stars melting into morning while singularly observing the crimson body of a lone velvety tree ant crawling up her long, tall back, in search of an easy meal.

Amira knows she is now a tree. There is no shock. No surprise. Only a feeling of contentment. A fluent understanding of time and place without the once restless pangs of examination. An overwhelming calm. Satiation of the soul. Amira didn't know this feeling existed. "Maybe I was always meant to be a tree." She thinks.

Noble fir.	Is she awake?
Redwood.	Yes.
Noble fir.	Why isn't she talking?
Redwood.	She's been through a lot. Relax.
Noble fir.	I'm just excited.
Redwood.	I know. But you need to settle down.
Noble fir.	Did she meet all three Straddlers?
Redwood.	She did.
Noble fir.	Must have been pretty confusing.

Redwood.   Yes.

Noble fir.   Should we tell her?

Redwood.   She knows.

Noble fir.   Will she be able to hear us?

Redwood.   Don't know.

Noble fir.   I really like her leaves. They're like, neon green.

Redwood.   Yes.

Amira can hear the trees talking about her. She is merely being polite. Amira can see she is surrounded by a handful of majestic specimens. Redwood. Madrone. Douglas fir. A smallish Noble fir. Honestly? She assumed there would be more to the smarter trees than this.

Amira.   So...

Redwood.   Good morning.

Amira.   Hi.

Noble fir.   I like your leaves. They're super green.

Amira.   Thank you.

Redwood.   How you doing?

Amira.   Good. Really good, actually.

Redwood.   Good. We'll let you rest.

Amira.   I'm not tired. Should I be?

Redwood.   Not necessarily.

Amira.   So...

Redwood.   Yes?

Amira.   What am I? What kind of tree?

Noble fir.   You're super tall.

Redwood.   You're a Sitka spruce.

Amira.   Oh. Okay.

Redwood.   Really good choice.

Amira.   Pardon me?

Redwood.   We all choose. Subconsciously.

Amira.   Weirdly, that makes sense.

Noble fir.   He planted all your books.

Amira.   Excuse me?

Redwood.   Nothing.

Noble fir.   The Straddler. He planted your books.

Amira.   Wait. What?

Redwood.   We can talk about this later.

Amira.   He *planted* the books?

Redwood.   It's a lot to take in. We'll let you rest.

Amira.   No way. Explain.

Noble fir.   She's feisty. I like her.

Amira.   Why would anyone plant a book?

Redwood.   Amira. Most of us were once books.

Amira.   Excuse me?

Redwood.   Most of the trees around here, were books.

Noble fir.   Not me. I'm just a tree.

Amira.   Wait... are you telling me... you were...

Redwood.   I was a book.

Amira.   But... I'm

Redwood.   You're a woman.

Amira.   Right.

Redwood.   Way better than a book.

Amira.   I'm lost.

Redwood.   Of course you are.

Amira.   So trees... everywhere... are books?

Redwood.   No.

Amira.   Just here.

Redwood.   Yes.

Amira.   Trees are just trees.

Redwood.   Yes.

Amira.   And they can talk.

Redwood.   Yes. But not all of them do.

Amira.   But the book thing?

Redwood.   Originally, every paper book was thought to have been destroyed. Assumption was, it didn't matter. The infinite capacity and universal access to the Collective made paper books an afterthought. But there was unseen energy hiding in paper books. By transforming the world's remaining books into trees, this energy was allowed to live on.

Amira.   I had the last nineteen books.

Redwood.   Yes.

Noble fir.   Women trees are super rare.

Redwood.   He's right.

Amira.   But there were tons of books written by -

Redwood.   Written by women?

Amira.   Yes.

Redwood.   None of them were saved.

Amira.   The nineteen I was protecting...

Redwood.   Written by men.

Amira.   So I'm...

Redwood.   You're the first tree created from a woman.

Noble fir.   We thought it was impossible.

Redwood.   We tried it once before. But...

Noble fir.   She was even more feisty than you.

Redwood.   It didn't work. Her name was Ellen.

Amira.   Wait. Ellen Kroptauer?

Redwood.   Yes.

Amira.   Krop.

Redwood.   Yes.

Amira.   So what does all this mean?

Redwood.   We don't know.

Amira.   Oh great.

Redwood.   We only know one thing.

Amira.   What?

Redwood.   You're part of the Potential.

Amira.   Which is?

Redwood.   We don't know.

Amira.   Wait... Oh no.

Noble fir.   What?

Amira.   No, no, no.

Noble fir.   What is it?

Amira.   The cutting. He was dying-

Redwood.   He's fine.

Noble fir.   He got planted down by the stream.

Amira.   He's alive?

Redwood.   Yes.

Amira.   Alluvial soil?

Redwood.   Yes.

Amira.   Will he become...

Redwood.   A full-grown tree?

Amira.   Yes.

Redwood.   It'll take a long time.

Amira.   So he wasn't a book.

Redwood.   No. He's a tree. A really good tree.

Amira.   But it's still him? He'll be the same?

Redwood.   Yes. Exactly the same. Just younger.

Noble fir.   Like me.

Redwood.   Yes. Young like you.

Amira.   So. How long do books take?

Redwood.   To grow into trees?

Amira.   Yeah.

Redwood.   Not as long as a seed. Or a cutting.

Amira.   But longer than humans.

Redwood.   Yes.

Amira.   Are there other... humans? Nearby?

Redwood.   No. You're the only one.

Amira.   How fun for me.

Redwood.   Amira?

Amira.   Yes?

Redwood.   No one's ever done what you did.

Amira.   What's that?

Noble fir. Become a full-grown tree in one night.

Redwood.   It's true. Never happened. That's how we knew.

Amira.   That I'm part of the Potential.

Redwood.   Yes.

Amira.   Yeah? Well what if I don't want to be?

Noble for. Oooh. Love her. So feisty.

Redwood.   Amira. You don't have to do anything.

Amira.   But I'm expected to do "something."

Redwood.   Not at all.

Amira.   Then what the booch does this all mean?

Redwood.   I told you. We don't know.

Amira.   Then how am I supposed to act?

Redwood.   Amira. This is about you, being you. That's it.

Amira.   But now I'm a booching tree.

Madrone.   Ahem.

Amira.   Yes?

Madrone.

Amira.   Excuse me?

Madrone.

Amira.	Were you gonna say something, or?

Madrone.

Amira.	I'm all ears.

Madrone.	You're not just a tree.

Amira.	Pardon?

Madrone.	You're *not* - just a tree.

Amira.	What does that mean?

Madrone.	You're a bet.

Amira.	A what?

Madrone.	A bet. Placed on the future.

Amira.	Oh great.

Madrone.	It is great.

Amira.	Why?

Madrone.	It means you're part of the Potential.

Amira.	I get all that. But the Potential of what?

Madrone.	We don't know exactly.

Amira.	Am I really hearing this?

Redwood.	Amira, please.

Amira.	You guys are supposed to be the smarter trees.

Madrone.	We have a theory.

Amira.	I'm listening.

Redwood.	You're part of the Potential... of...

Amira.	Yes.

Madrone.	The Potential of good.

Amira.   Which means?

Madrone.   A manifested hope. For all that is possible.

Amira.   As a tree.

Madrone.   And a woman.

Amira.   How?

Madrone.   We don't know.

Amira.   Are you kidding me? That's the theory?

Redwood.   Amira?

Amira.   This is *nuts.*

Redwood.   Amira. Listen to me. What do you feel?

Amira.   Feel? Right this second?

Redwood.   Yes. Right now. What do you feel?

Amira.   I feel pressure. Pressure to be someone I'm not.

Redwood.   How did you feel when you first knew?

Amira.   First knew what?

Redwood.   That you were a tree.

Amira.   I felt...

Redwood.   Yes?

Amira.   I felt amazing. Then I talked to you guys.

Noble fir. Ha. She was good until she met us.

Redwood.   But the initial feeling? The first thing?

Amira.   Initially? I felt like I was - home.

Madrone.   Exactly.

Amira.   What is that supposed to mean?

Madrone.   You just need a little time.

144

Amira.   Yeah? What if time doesn't help?

Madrone.   It will. Shhh…

Redwood.   Someone's coming.

Amira.   What? Who?

Redwood.   Quiet.

Madrone.   Shhhhh…

Noble fir.

Amira.

Redwood.

Madrone.

Noble fir.

There's a sharp rustling among the understory bushes of goatsbeard and wood sorrel. It abruptly stops. Starts. Stops again. The sound isn't at all exploratory. It's almost mechanical. Then. Strutting out of the bushes. Silent grace and power. Unmistakable. A large, muscular, sleek, tawny grey puma. A mountain lion. Weaving through the smarter trees like a deliberate spirit. Wandering. Perusing. Circling Amira like a goddess with an agenda.

Puma.   Hello, Amira.

Amira.

Puma.   I know you can hear me.

Amira.

Puma.   Amira?

Amira.

Puma.   I can wait all day, if you'd like.

Amira.   Feel free to chime in anytime, guys.

Puma.   The trees can't hear you now, Amira.

Amira.   Sure they can. They're just startled.

Puma.   Why would trees be startled, Amira?

Amira.   Because you're a mountain lion.

Puma.   And, why would trees care about this?

Amira.   Well.

Puma.   Trees can only hear certain things, Amira.

Amira.   Okay.

Puma.   Women, can hear much more.

Amira.   So... You're a woman?

Puma.   Just like you.

Amira.   And?

Puma.   You've been chosen. Just like me.

Amira.   Lucky us.

Puma.   Wow. How long have you been a tree?

Amira.   Look. What do you want?

Puma.   You're already restless.

Amira.   I'm not restless. I'm just...

Puma.   Resentful? Angry? Frightened?

Amira.   Whoa-whoa-whoa.

Puma.   Hit a nerve?

Amira.   Hardly. I don't even know you.

Puma.   Ha. I was exactly like you.

146

Amira.   Doubt it.

Puma.   Ha ha. Brings back memories.

Amira.   So you're better than me?

Puma.   Ha ha ha. You're delightful.

Amira.   Will you just leave me alone, please?

Puma.   Amira, you don't get it, do you.

Amira.   What am I supposed to *get?*

Puma.   This isn't about you. It's about everything else. Everything "other" than you, Amira. When you focused on helping others, did you notice that the focus on "you" disappeared? Confusion can't exist in the presence of purpose. The feeling you first experienced during your transformation into a tree. What was that like?

Amira.   Incredible. I could see - and feel - everything.

Puma.   Exactly. And within no time at all, you're losing that perspective. Same thing happened to me. First few moments into my transformation, I had vision like I'd never experienced. I could feel every vibration. Every sensation was fine-tuned and perfect. Massive yet visceral. As if it were all hand-made for me. But the hardest part to learn? It wasn't made for me. None of it. It's about everything else. Everything other than self. A vast, deep, selfless connection to good. With the ability to see and interpret totality from a distance.

Amira.   So then where does it come from?

Puma.   No one knows.

Amira.   Then how do you know it's good?

Puma.   You felt it, didn't you?

Amira.   I used to feel good when I juiced.

Puma.   Amira.

Amira.   I'm serious.

Puma.   You're part of an invisible chain, Amira. An invisible current that literally, flows through everything. This chain, if it's able to remain intact, keeps the potential for good alive in everything. Without this chain? Good, dies.

Amira.   Pretty dark.

Puma.   Over time, the chain has grown dramatically weaker. One of the initial theories as to the decline in the quality of the chain? Not enough problem-solvers. Scientists. Chemists. Engineers. Biologists. Inventors. Easy enough. Recruit the best and insert them into the chain. This worked beautifully for a while. The majority of the world's biggest issues were suddenly being solved. This is how the Collective was born.

Amira.   The Collective? I don't follow.

Puma.   It was surmised that if we could somehow create the ability to seamlessly share ideas between humans, we could dramatically accelerate problem-solving.

Amira.   And?

Puma.   Worked brilliantly. The Collective allowed data and ideation to, literally, flow through everyone. With nonstop access to a constantly-evolving fountain of human input, it was assumed the chain would only grow stronger.

Amira.   But?

Puma.   While the big problems were being fixed, the little things, the unseen things, were quickly imploding.

Amira.   Like?

Puma.   People started becoming one-dimensional. As you may have noticed, this paradigm continues today. What was once hailed as a universal connection between everyone, ultimately lead to the destruction of individuality.

Amira.   But people are still using the Collective.

Puma.   They're using data. Not the Collective. Once the world's biggest problems were solved, the original intent of the Collective was lost. Benevolent connection became irrelevant.

Amira.   So, what became of the invisible chain?

Puma.   The chain grew critically weak.

Amira.   And?

Puma.   Enter the second wave of transformation.

Amira.   Is this where we are now?

Puma.   No. The second wave supposed we were lacking in philosophic discourse. The freedom to discuss philosophical ideas without a thirst for universal agreement. Thus, we sought purveyors of rhetorical wisdom. The deep thinkers.

Amira.   This can't be where I come in.

Puma.   This is where I came in.

Amira.   Ah.

Puma.   The first wave of transformation strength-
ened the chain by solving the big problems with scientific
pragmatism. The second wave was thought to be needed to
add a reinforced layer of idealistic pragmatism. An amalgam
of idealistic dreams, woven with strong threads of utilitarian
reasoning.

Amira.   Sounds logical.

Puma.   It was.

Amira.   So?

Puma.   It wasn't enough.

Amira.   Why not?

Puma.   Well. Let's see. How do I explain it in really
simple terms? When a group of intellectuals get together to
dance? They tend to dance in a vacuum.

Amira.   I can't picture a group of intellectuals dancing.

Puma.   Exactly. Thus? Today, we enter the third wave.

Amira.   Is this where I come in?

Puma.   Maybe.

Amira.   Why do I feel you've chosen poorly?

Puma.   Probably.

Amira.   Thanks.

Puma.   Amira, choosing you was not an accident.

This isn't a choice based on your ability to single-handedly solidify the chain. This is a bet placed on empirical evidence. Watching you over time has revealed something we all realized was missing.

Amira.   Which is?

Puma.   You won't like it.

Amira.   The fact that I stopped dating?

Puma.   Amira.

Amira.   Horrifying.

Puma.   It's incredibly simple, but infinitely complex.

Amira.   Okay.

Puma.   "Curiosity."

Amira.   Wait... what?

Puma.   Exactly.

Amira.   I'm lost.

Puma.   Amira. You are blessed with eternal hunger.

A perpetual, heartfelt angst. In its simplest form, curiosity. A beautiful, yet impossibly-insatiable thirst for all things unknowable.

Amira.   Wow. That's kind of insulting.

Puma.   Said you wouldn't like it.

Amira.   So this chain...

Puma.   Yes?

Amira.   How do we know it actually exists?

Puma.   It's a feeling. That's all it is.

Amira.   A feeling?

Puma.   Yes.

Amira.   But you said you were 'watching' me.

Puma.   Feeling is seeing, Amira. Feeling is the only true way of seeing. Our eyes deceive us. Our ears play tricks. Taste leads us astray. Smell distracts. Feeling always reveals our purest vision.

Amira.   Wait. Can't a feeling be wrong?

Puma.   If you allow it to be.

Amira.   Can I ask you something?

Puma.   Of course.

Amira.   There are a lot of "curious" people.

Puma.   Why choose you?

Amira.   Yeah. Why me?

Puma.   Do you really want to know?

Amira.   Of course.

Puma.   You've always been different, Amira. You never quite fit. You knew this from an early age. Yet you kept on searching for clues. Answers. And when you didn't find these answers, you didn't give up. You remained infinitely flexible. Through your darkest moments you managed to put other's needs before your own. You always found ways to help, Amira. Always without any need for you to benefit personally. You fiercely protected the curiosity of others. You made sure there was ample room for their curiosity to grow.

You never took, Amira. You only gave. Even now. This very moment. Your becoming a tree. As magical as it all seems? Like some sort of spiritual payoff? Even with all the thoughts spinning inside you about what it all means. Know one thing, Amira. This wasn't a gift to you. This was a gift to everything else. And as crazy as it all seems, we have no idea what it means right now. We may never know. We can only know how it feels. And with every new day. If we're lucky. We'll feel it. All of us. Even you.

Amira.　　　Why do I doubt everything you just said?

Puma.　　　The weight of responsibility you're experiencing is expected. But not necessary. No one expects anything from you, Amira. The sad truth? No one cares. No one is even paying attention. Everyone is busy chasing their own ephemeral dreams. The pressure isn't on you, Amira. Because the pressure doesn't exist. Even if you were to decide to become a conscious force against good, it wouldn't matter. There's way too much momentum behind self. Ego is the new master. The energy required to shift this, is unimaginable. But the idea of not trying? The idea of ignoring the obvious decay of idealogical social benevolence and the latent power of good? Not an option. You may act as a conduit, Amira. Maybe a catalyst. Perhaps this deeply curious love inside you will serve as fuel for others. Invisible food for lost souls. That's the essence of the Potential. No one is looking at you to be a savior, Amira. The energy hiding inside trees and paper books is real. But the energy hiding inside a well-meaning woman, is immeasurable. That's why you were chosen. To continue being the unique, loving, curious soul you already are. That's it, Amira.

With these final words, the mountain lion gazes up to the changing sky above Amira's long, magnificent branches. Blinks her piercing, smiling eyes. And gracefully walks away.

Oblivious to the conversation that has just taken place, the smarter trees pick up exactly where they left off.

Redwood. I'm sure I heard something.

Madrone. Must have been a deer.

Noble fir. Didn't sound like a deer.

Madrone. I forget what we were talking about.

Redwood. You were advising Amira to take her time.

Madrone. Right, right.

Redwood. She's feeling incredible pressure.

Madrone. Yes. Indeed. I remember now.

Noble fir. Amira, you've got like a million birds on you.

Amira. I see that.

Noble fir. I don't get many birds.

Amira. Why not?

Noble fir. Um. I think I'm too dense?

Amira. Ah. Not enough open spaces?

Noble fir. I get lots of chipmunks.

Amira.   That sounds fun.

Noble fir.   Yeah. They're pretty funny.

Redwood.   Would you like to talk more, Amira?

Amira.   About?

Madrone.   The pressure you're under.

Redwood.   Being new to the Potential and all.

Amira.   I think I'm good.

Madrone.   Oh.

Redwood.   Wow. Um. Okay.

Madrone.   So glad we could help.

Amira.   Yes. Thank you so much. For helping.

Hundreds of birds flitter about within Amira's long arms, warming their chests in the last drops of sunlight. Amira giggles as the birds tickle her skin with their needle-sharp toes.

Amira has an epiphany. "Maybe the smarter trees are the trees who never say a word. Maybe the world is filled with smarter trees. Maybe they simply prefer to remain quiet. *Feel* instead of talk. Maybe the world's trees know that wisdom is energy. To be eternally held. Shared. Protected. Savored. All done invisibly. Maybe the world's trees hold a vast, universal secret. And now, I get to play a part."

Night arrives without any agenda. "This will be a big job." Amira thinks. "To see everything. Yet remain merely curious." Then all at once, she remembers. "This isn't a job. It's a gift." And for the first time, Amira feels lucky to have been chosen.

Amira glances up and notices stars being ripped apart and squeezed together. She watches new stars being born. Old stars collapsing and dying. The energy required for this is inconceivable. Impossible for even the smartest tree to comprehend. Yet even the youngest sapling is able to view the sparkling heavens with awe and wonder.

"Potential is ceaseless." Amira thinks. "Even within the darkest vacuum of nothingness. Even when all the world's biggest problems have been solved. Even when people trade away individuality and compassion for a few sips of data."

"Potential is everything." Amira thinks. And for the first time, she can literally, feel it. This is the last thought Amira has before she drifts off to sleep.

Amira begins to dream a familiar dream. She is fully aware she's dreaming. Amira begins to giggle. Once again she is rolling down a hillside meadow of lupine and creamcups. But something is different. Children are rolling through the meadow with her. Laughing. Giggling louder than she. Collectively welcoming the prickly caress of flowers brushing against their unprotected hands and faces. This is when Amira realizes she is not actually in the meadow. Or watching the meadow from afar. She is the meadow itself. "I am many things." Amira thinks. "A meadow. A tree. A woman. A feeling. I am the Potential."

www.ingramcontent.com/pod-product-compliance
Lightning Source LLC
Chambersburg PA
CBHW050145110726
47898CB00008B/2675